"Parker's a cur!"

Stingaree said with great excitement. "I've trailed him for three thousand miles. I've run him down. I tell you there would be no charge laid against me. Everybody in Fort Anxious knows that he's hired men to kill me. Everybody knows that he's probably trying to kill me now. Don't you see how simple it is?"

His face hardened on a smile.

"But that would be murder," the girl said.

"Not murder. Duty. Bob Dillman was the straightest friend that any man ever had."

THE STINGAREE
was originally published by Dodd, Mead & Company.

Other books by Max Brand

The
Stingaree

MAX BRAND

PUBLISHED BY POCKET BOOKS NEW YORK

THE STINGAREE

Dodd, Mead edition published August, 1968
Pocket Book edition published November, 1970

This *Pocket Book* edition includes every word
contained in the original, higher-priced edition. It is printed
from brand-new plates made from completely reset, clear, easy-to-read
type. *Pocket Book* editions are published by Pocket Books, a division
of Simon & Schuster, Inc., 630 Fifth Avenue, New York, N.Y. 10020.
Trademarks registered in the United States and other countries.

Standard Book Number: 671-55080-2.
Library of Congress Catalog Card Number: 68-23092.
This **Pocket Book** edition is published by arrangement with
Dodd, Mead & Company.

Printed in the U.S.A.

The
Stingaree

CHAPTER ONE

IN THE GOOD old sententious style, there is the saying: "He is two men who has two languages." Jimmy Green had three. He drove dogs in French-Canadian; he hunted in Cree; but he fought in English. He had other talents. He was only five feet and five and a half inches tall, but he could march on snowshoes with any man; he could shoot off the head of a red squirrel as it peeked among the upper branches of a great pine tree; he could make his own moccasins; he could skin a caribou, cure a beaver pelt, and trap a fox; and it was even said of him by the Crees—though this was perhaps more compliment than truth: "He can hunt moose!" Also, he could run like an Indian, use a knife like a Canuck, and hit like a white man with a straight-driving fist.

He was thirteen years old, and at that age, the Canadians forgave him for being an American. His parents, when Jimmy Green was two, had barely finished building a cabin on the side of Mount Crozier when an avalanche jumped down its side and pushed mother and father Green, their house, their household goods, their three dogs, their mule, and their string of traps into Lake Anxious. When the rescuers climbed up the hillside, they found two lives rubbed out, and the two-year-old sitting in the snow and laughing at the world.

He had kept on laughing ever since, and he had a good many reasons. The people of Fort Anxious adopted him. Not the Canadians alone, but the half-breeds, the random American traders with their red noses and long drawls, all the visitors, and even the Indians themselves. He was a part of the town and he belonged to it as a beaver belongs to its family.

When his toes were frostbitten and he hungered for sweet pemmican, he condescended to go to the house of the good old priest, Father Pierre, and there he was taught reading and writing and pushed gently along the road of learning; but his usual interests lay in other quarters. He used to be seen as a mere infant seated on the floor of a Cree lodge with his teeth fastened in a chunk of moose meat from which he patiently sawed off a bite with a knife a foot long. Then he learned to climb the stages and steal meat from them. There was not a man in the village who had not reached for him with a heavy boot.

Since the whole town was his mother, every one had to feed and clothe and amuse and cherish Jimmy Green. Since the entire fort was his father, every man who wanted to could discipline Jimmy; it was only necessary to catch him first, which was not much more difficult than to lay hands on something which possessed the mingled virtues and vices of a fisher, a greyhound, and a fox. When caught, he was all teeth and claws, but nevertheless, he received some hearty thrashings. He used to bawl out and whoop and scream in his misery in order to shorten these punishments, until one day— he was being flogged for stealing the whole of a great venison pie!—a Cree passed by and seeing what was happening, quickly lowered his head and strode away. After that, Jimmy Green never cried again.

He was all tooth and claw, hard muscle, and sharp wits. He had followed the wise trail of the grizzly and pursued the devious way of Reynard, the fox. He had seen otters fish and squirrels climb. He had watched the snowshoe rabbit run and the eagle soar. Indian boys had taught him how to steal; Indian braves had taught him how to hunt and how to endure the pinch of hunger and weariness. Wrestling, fighting, wrangling, bargaining, shooting, and truth-telling on important occasions, he knew from the whites. Therefore, his education was quite complete. He would have been at home in a New York slum, in a sailing ship's forecastle, a Texas desert, or on a cake of ice. In a word, he was blamed and loved for every stroke of mischief in Fort Anxious.

He was not poor but had accumulated a treasure upon which he would not have known how to put a price. He had an old rifle which had been given him by a retiring trader at the fort; he had a knife which had been solemnly willed to him by François le Beau on his deathbed. He kept a leather sling, and a rubber-strung slingshot. He had twenty-seven marbles, one clouded agate, and one clear. He owned, furthermore, a broken awl, a one-legged pocketknife, a silver spoon with the brass showing through only in spots, half of a rawhide lariat, a working collar for a dog, a moosehide whip, a twist of wood that looked like a revolver, and a leaden horse with a leaden rider which only lacked a head to be perfect.

He loved an old man, a young man, and a girl.

The old man was Father Pierre, of course; the young man was Awaskees, the strong Cree who sometimes allowed him to go along on the moose hunt. But the secret love, the consuming desire, the profound emotion of his life, was Miss Paula Carson. She was twenty years old, as brown as a beaver, as rosy as a crushed berry, as delightful as a June day, and her smile and her pleasant laughter so dwelled in the mind of our hero that sometimes after he had gone to bed he lay with pain and yearning puckering his brow and could not sleep for five minutes, or even ten.

In all the world there was only one thing which Jimmy Green really hated, and that was the long, clear mirror which hung over the fireplace in the best room of the priest's house, for in time he saw that his nose was short—stumpy, in fact! —and that it was more speckled than a trout. He could not help seeing, also, that his eyes were not set off by the penciling of brows; that lashes there appeared to be none, and that his bright eyes were of no particular color, but gray, green, washed-out blue, or pale amber, according as the light struck them. When he saw this face of his, Miss Paula Carson seemed farther removed from him. But he scorned doubt! And every time when he returned from the priest's house to wherever he was making his home, he carefully looked through his list of treasures and told himself that he was a man.

On this morning he rose to work. His job was the taming of a huge hundred-and-sixty-pound beast which was nine tenths wolf and the other tenth dynamite, and gentling this monster so that it would stand in harness and not try to take off the leg of every creature that passed by. It was called a Mackenzie husky, but the boy was sure that it was misnamed, for it had the look, the talents, and the tameless ferocity of a timber wolf.

These qualities in it did not overawe the boy. He was merely annoyed by them, but was determined to win the battle, for he had been promised by Kite Larkin ten cents and an old pair of fur mittens from which only the thumbs and the finger tips had been worn away.

On his way down from the attic, he prepared himself for the battle by practicing his most formidable scowl. He had his moosehide whip in his hand, the butt of it loaded with leaden shot, the thong coiled around his arm. When he went out to see the dog, it greeted him by leaping to the end of its chain, a section of which it had been polishing with patient chewing, for hours on hours. Jimmy Green was well inside of its leaping distance, but he measured the target perfectly and crashed the heavy butt of the whip with all his might squarely between the eyes of Mishe Mukwa. That is Ojibway for "grizzly bear," and the dog got his name from the bear look of his short, furry ears, and a misguiding expression of mingled wisdom and humor which sat in his face. Jim had shortened this name to Mishie, and the name stuck.

That club stroke dropped Mishe Mukwa senseless to the ground, after which the boy hitched a muzzle to the great head, unhooked the chain from the big iron staple to which it was anchored, and when Mishie wakened with a snarl, he herded the big brute before him to the street. Mishe Mukwa wanted to turn and fight. He champed until foam flew from his curling lips. His eyes turned red. His mane lifted. To the boy, he looked as big as his namesake. But still Jimmy enjoyed this daily walk, for on every hand eyes glanced at him and heads nodded, as much as to say: "The kid is growing up!"

He steered Mishie into the lodge of the first Cree family that neighbored the street. Grandmother, mother, two or three tough-bodied youngsters, and a crawling infant were in the tepee. But the boy went in with the huge dog and stood by the meat pot which hung over the central fire. From this he helped himself plentifully. The whole Cree family began to scream at him. The grandmother rescued the baby from the floor, the wolf dog kicked over a back rest and began to howl.

"I don't hear you," said the boy patiently.

That was almost true, because the dog was making enough noise to drown even war whoops. So Jimmy Green remained in that lodge until he had eaten his fill, and then he departed, unmolested.

He walked on, fingering the weight of the loaded whip-end, and seeing before him Sam Ward in company with a sturdy half-breed boy, he loftily prepared to receive their admiration of the size of Mishie and his own dauntless courage in attempting to subdue such a brute. But they came on with heads close together, unseeing, as it appeared. They did not even hear his salutation, but as they went by the half-breed was saying with unnecessary loudness:

"What's a pug nose good for?"

"Aw," said Sam, "it's handy to hang a hat on!"

CHAPTER TWO

THE DIGNITY of Jimmy Green was not to be lightly taken.

What he heard from the pair of them made his head swim. It was as though his innumerable battles with sticks, stones, and fists had been no more than the triumphs of dreams. It was as though some other lad in Fort Anxious were able to run faster, shoot straighter, hit harder.

He turned, infuriated as he realized that all these things were true about himself alone. He shouted in a ringing voice:

"Hey, Sammy! Hey, Sam!"

But Sam and the half-breed walked on, their heads close together, still enchanted, as it were, by the same topic.

"What is a pug nose good for?"

Jimmy Green, breathing very hard, stared after them for some time. He could not understand it. Was not this his town? According to his royal pleasure the lives of boys became acceptable or noxious. Even the sons of the richest men at the fort hastened at the call of Jimmy Green.

Slowly, therefore, he wondered what madness could have possessed Sam Ward, otherwise not an unworthy boy. And he turned upon his bare foot again, grimly promising to himself the luxury and the delight of knocking holes through Sammy.

Ahead, he heard an outbreak of violent voices, turning a corner. They were on his side of the street. Young Jimmy turned instantly to the farther side. He kicked the ribs of the wolf dog and whanged him two or three times with the loaded butt of the whip just to assure the brute that he, Jimmy Green, was on hand and was master.

The cause which made the dog skulk so far away now came around the corner. Jimmy saw in the lead four trappers, the sweeping manes and tails of their horses braided with stained shells, with feathers, and with glittering trinkets; and their clothes, especially the soft deerskin trousers, covered with decorations. They wore long hair that swept about their shoulders. Their hats were off and hanging on the sides of their saddles. Their horses were not large, but finely formed, with eyes that shone with high spirits and mischief—true mustangs. Every movement they made flashed with their golden and silver ornaments.

The boy could have stood and enjoyed the sight of them, another day. He could even have run along beside them and laughed and joked with them. But now it was very different, for he had with him a thing which every eye in that train could appraise and rightly value—such a dog as never had leaned against a collar in any freight train that ever hauled over the winter snows into Fort Anxious. So he kept the dog well to one side on short chain as the cavalcade went by.

They saw him at once. Or rather, they saw the dog, and they came with a whoop. They could take now, and pay next winter. That was their usual system! They came yelling. They raced for a prize, and the first one to touch the dog would be its owner. That agreement was understood as they jammed the spurs into their horses.

Young Jimmy Green looked at them as if they had been so many fiends leaning over the pommels of their saddles. But, as they came nearer, while Jimmy was still wondering whether or not he should try to use his knife, or simply let the dog go with them, they sat up in their saddles and split to either side of him as water splits against a rock. They dashed by with shouts and with loud laughter, making a great joke of this affair, but the boy guessed that their mirth was an afterthought. He turned, and he saw behind him the Cree, Awaskees, smiling gently, a rifle lying carelessly across the hollow of his left arm.

"Thank you, Father," said Jimmy Green in Cree.

Awaskees muttered something which cannot be translated in the whole, but which meant: "May there always be fire in your lodge, a filled meat pot over the fire, tobacco in your pipe, smoke in your nose, and a fat dog for your squaw to roast!"

This very inclusive "good morning" was given as Awaskees stepped on across the street, and no one uninitiated could have guessed that his coming up behind the boy had been intentional, or that his rifle had split that gay charge of dog thieves. However, Jimmy Green knew very well, and he looked after the soft-stepping Cree and vowed that he would remember.

He had barely turned the next corner when, with a series of war whoops, a crowd of a dozen boys boiled out of an alley, dragging another youngster in their midst. He hesitated, ready to drop even the chain of the dog and flee at full speed; but as the boys came nearer, he could see that they were members of his own "tribe," of which he was the undisputed chief. He was seen. They poured toward him.

"Hey, look, Jimmy! Look what we got! We got Mickey Dugan. He was clean across to our side of the bridge. Hey, Jimmy, whacha think? We're gunna scalp him and give him a ducking!"

Mickey Dugan, ragged, almost, as Jimmy himself, was one of the leading spirits of the tribe which represented the other half of the town. His capture was no small event, and Mickey bore himself very well, head high, disdainful, but a little green in the face. To be "scalped" was not actually to have the hair of his head removed, but the process was almost as painful and as long remembered. To be ducked was, for such a strong boy, almost to be drowned. It was a great victory, but something in the eye of Mickey held the attention of Jimmy.

"What was he doing?" he asked.

"He was—whacha think?—fishin' behind Mrs. Villar's house. Tryin' to sneak some fish out of our side of the river!"

Jimmy stepped closer to Mickey and looked him in the eye. And Mickey looked dauntlessly back. Thrice they had fought. Victory had been undecided twice. Once, because Mickey's father had lurched out and kicked him homeward; once, because Jimmy's crowd had charged. And the third time victory had inclined to Jimmy's side, but it had cost him a large, beautiful eye which still was represented by a faint purple line. However, the soul of Jimmy was just.

"Hey, Mickey," said he, "whacha come fishin' on our side of the river for, hey?"

"None of your dang business," said Mickey, "and if I had my hands loose, I'd black up both your eyes."

Jimmy moistened his lips with the tip of his tongue. But he merely said again: "What sentcha over to our side of the river this time of day when you might've knowed that we'd see you?"

This challenge launched against his intelligence stung Mickey to answer.

"The old man wanted fish for breakfast, and he give me

13

five minutes or a lickin'. They ain't bitin' on our side, this time of the day!"

"Humph!" said Jimmy, and shifted from one foot to the other. With all his soul he yearned to see this great and dangerous enemy scalped and ducked, but something raised in his eye the brutal picture of Mickey's drunken father.

"He sent you out to catch fish, eh? Where's your line?"

Mickey disdained answer.

"I got it," admitted a wide-shouldered clansman. "I seen him first. It belongs to me by rights."

"Give it back to him," said Jimmy slowly.

The other quailed, and producing the precious string and hook, held it forth. Jimmy took it.

"Leave his hands go," said Jimmy.

A wild uproar arose. They protested that it was a fair capture. They demanded justice.

"Whacha mean?" yelled Jimmy, pink with rage. "Didn't his old man send him? Ain'tcha got no sense? Leave his hands go, I say!"

They loosed his hands. If they obeyed Jimmy, it was because they knew the weight of his fists.

"Here's your line," said Jimmy Green. "G'wan and get, will ya? Hey, Louis! G'wan and get your fish spear, will ya, and give him a hand. His old man sent him. You don't want Mickey licked for nothin', do ya?"

CHAPTER THREE

STERNLY, Jimmy stood by and saw justice done. By the gloomy faces of his band he could guess that his authority was strained to the uttermost by the act. However, the hearts of kings are made large to endure the pain of all their subjects, together with their own woes, so Jimmy endured, and watched Mickey taken off to liberty and the bridge, and little Louis, the dexterous fisherman, scampering beside him.

Big Mishe Mukwa, as though realizing that something of importance was toward, lay down, in the meantime, without making any of his usual frantic efforts to escape, and regarded his young trainer with his head canted a bit to one side and the most doggish expression that the boy ever had seen on his face.

He saw Mishe Mukwa, and he also saw, looking through a close-grown pair of poplars, the brown, smiling face of Paula Carson. She came out from between the trees, smiling. The brightness of morning was in her face—of an autumn morning, say, because such beauty surely cannot last!

"Hullo," said Paula Carson, "where'd you get the dog, Jimmy?"

"I got it off of Kite Larkin."

"What's his name?"

"Mishe Mukwa."

"Why, that's Ojibway for 'grizzly,' isn't it?"

"Yeah. Well, you look at him, he's kind of that way around the head and shoulders."

She looked; she circled. Mishe rose and snarled and erected his mane with savage hate.

"He's not very gentlemanly yet," said Paula Carson gravely. "You'll most certainly have to teach him good manners, Jimmy."

"Yeah! Won't I, though!"

"What will Kite give you?"

"Aw, I dunno, Paula. He promised me ten cents and a pair of old mittens."

"The contemptible—" began Paula, and changed smoothly to: "Well, that's worth having, Jimmy. But you'll be careful of yourself with him? He looks like a terror!"

"Him? He ain't nothin'," said Jimmy, with rather overdone contempt. "I gotta loaded whip-butt, here, and he knows what it tastes like."

"I saw Father Pierre the other day."

"Yeah?" said Jimmy guiltily.

"He said that you haven't been for a week to take a lesson."

Jimmy jerked up his head and turned crimson with excitement.

"Listen, Paula," said he, "d'you want me to go there?"

"Of course I do," said she.

"I'll go every day, or bust," said Jimmy desperately. He perspired. "Beginnin' the week after next," said he. "Awaskees is gunna show me some trap makin'," he explained weakly.

"I'll have to go along," said Paula.

He wanted her to say something about his recent act of

justice. Did she, perhaps, take it for cowardice? Was that why she had been smiling so broadly.

"Hey, Paula," he exclaimed.

She turned back. "Yes, Jimmy?"

"Hey, you know old man Beeson's gone and got himself a new squaw. Whacha think of that!"

"I've heard about it," said she, and would have turned away again, but once more he stopped her.

"Hey, Paula!"

She came deliberately back to him, studying him.

"What do you want to tell me, Jimmy?" she asked.

He was troubled by this prescience. It was not the first time that he had encountered it in her.

"I wanted to know, Paula," said he, "would you think I was scared of that Mickey was why I let him go?"

"Jimmy," she answered, "a good judge always trusts his own opinion."

She left him, and he went on his way out of town, wondering if there had been a faint beginning of a smile on her lips. Besides, he could not tell exactly what she meant. But that, he decided, was one reason why he loved her, for she was ever the unsolvable problem.

Outside the town, he halted at the verge of the big trees and looked back across the familiar landscape, for it was never so well known to him that he did not wish for the eye of a hawk as he stared down. He saw a thick column of smoke rising from the house of Dugan, and guessed by this that Louis' spear had been instantly successful in the river.

Yonder in Lake Anxious floated a stationary boat, a moveless figure, and the sun striking a thin, curved line of light from the rod. And still farther away a canoe with two paddlers and a hump of goods in the center of the boat, shot out from the white smothers of the rapids and swept down the central current. He stood tiptoe, so anxiously did he strain his eyes toward them. From a great distance, no doubt, they were bringing furs, and he could almost feel beneath his finger tips the rich pelage of marten, ermine, beaver, and fox. Then he turned into the trees.

For he knew that the wolf dog would be more at home among the shadows. Instantly, the dog's carriage changed. He walked lightly, on his toes. His head lowered almost as though he were stalking, and his glance at the boy made Jimmy Green think of the side-rip of a fighting wolf.

However, no matter how dangerous the big fellow might be, he meant both money and reputation to Jimmy Green, so the boy set to work. He had two main methods. One was to strap a small load on the back of the wolf dog, then lead it along. The second was to stand behind it and try to induce it to pull forward. He could manage the first thing fairly well, because Mishe knew the meaning of the whip, but the moment he tried to get behind the husky, Mishe would whirl about, trying to free his powerful jaws.

It was nervous, exacting work. Already, he had spent three days on the monster and felt that he had made almost no progress, but he stuck doggedly at it. Now, they drifted through the grove in which they were at practice and came out from the trees onto a pleasant hill shoulder beyond the woods. There the sun came with delightful strength against the breast and the face of the boy. The grass at his feet was stirring and flashing in the wind, and the smell of green growing things came over him with a drowsy sweetness. To breathe of this air was as good as moose meat and bear's fat. And young Jimmy Green tilted back his head a little in excess of comfort.

He looked down to Mishe and would have given a great deal to know what the husky knew as it stood with head high and eyes tightly closed, reading the wind with its wise nose. Out of the thicket, then, a partridge darted and shot over the meadow with a loud thrumming, a mere dark spot, obscured by a mist of rapid wings.

Instead of a dog chain, ah, for a shotgun in hand then! The partridge shot upward as it neared the boy. It was at the height of its rise when a gun boomed short and deep on the edge of the opposite woods, and the big bird tipped over and bumped solidly upon the ground.

Agape, Jimmy stared, for this was not the sound of a shotgun; and now he saw on the edge of the stalwart line of tree trunks a tall man in whose hand a revolver winked as he put it away quickly beneath his coat. There was something unhurried about that movement, like the inescapable reach of a cat's paw, and Jimmy Green was fascinated. Moreover, this was shooting that he had seen. He knew distances. He could swear it was forty yards from the trees to the spot where the partridge had fallen, and though every man in Fort Anxious would swear that this was a lucky shot, Jimmy suddenly and devoutly knew that it was not. The moment that hand slid for a gun the bird had been as good as dead.

Now he stepped forth from the tree shadows, a tall man, with wide shoulders, smiling a little, and waving his hand slowly and gracefuly toward the boy. And the heart of Jimmy Green enlarged, as once it had done in the woods when he saw the great dark body of a moose lifting from among a grove of willows. He had seen larger men. In that Northland, men, like trees and like bears, grow big; they need size for their work, it would seem.

Yet never had he felt this instant impression of power adequate to every need. No sense of audience seemed to move in this big, slow-stepping fellow. His smile was perfectly genial, and yet like the wind he carried with him a sense of the mysterious horizon, and the other side of the world.

CHAPTER FOUR

HE SO IMPRESSED the boy that even a seasoned hunter like Jimmy Green neglected to look at his clothes at first. Yet they were worth a great deal of attention, as a matter of fact. They were very battered and tattered. Ten thousand miles of walking could not have given to his trousers an effect other than that of the trousers of a horseman. His boots, too, looked cramped and pointed like a rider's boots, and the loose brim of his hat, one felt, had been unhinged by flapping up and down against the wind of a brisk gallop.

This was the appearance of the stranger, not touching on such minor things as coat sleeves worn out at the elbows, and not even a sign of a pack at his back. You might have said that he was out enjoying a promenade, for all the baggage he carried with him. There was only one explanation in the eye of Jimmy, and that was that he was a voyageur who had been overturned in shooting some rapids. Yet he was not the voyageur type. He wore not the same clothes. He had not about him a vestige of the northern environment. The very color of his skin was more richly brown, as though darkened on purpose to turn the edge of a very sharp, keen sun.

This stranger, walking across the meadow, picked up the partridge and walked on, but to the amazement of the boy, he kept a path turning away from Jimmy Green! As though, marvelous to say, he was not one of ordinary mortals, who rejoice to meet strangers in the wilderness.

"Hello!" sang out Jimmy.

"Hello!" said the cheerful stranger.

And, with a nod and a smile, he walked on, carrying the limp partridge, whose wings fell down like cups to either side.

"That ain't the Fort Anxious trail!" offered the boy.

"Isn't it?" asked the other. "Where does it lie, then, brother?"

"Yonder," said Jimmy.

"How far, can you tell me?"

"Might be coupla mile, I guess."

"Ah," said the big stranger. "Then I might as well have dinner here. Will you join me?"

As he spoke, he slipped to the ground at the side of a tall, thick shrub, and reaching behind him, he broke off a few handfuls of the dried, dead branches. It seemed plain that his intention was to build a fire at his very feet—yes, or between them!

Jimmy Green drew nearer.

He had seen Indian braves on the warpath, a wolverene breaking up a line of traps, the Mackenzie in spring flood smashing its ice barriers, and Awaskees hunting moose; but never had he seen that which intrigued him more than the stranger from the South. From no other direction could he have come!

He did not need a second or a stronger invitation. No matter how backward Jimmy might be with strangers, he advanced cheerfully, though with a woodsman's caution. The wolf dog, smelling warm blood, lurched forward with a mumbling in his throat. The jar nearly jerked Jimmy's arm out by the roots, when he heard the man saying calmly:

"Let him step right along. Always had a likin' for dogs. Reach him right here to me, sonny!"

His pronunciation, even, differed from that of other men. It could have been spelled: "A'ways had a lahkin' foh dawgs. Reach 'm raht heah t'me, sonny." It fascinated Jimmy still more and more to listen to these words, spoken in a soft, deep voice.

"You mean you wanta have me let him go?" asked Jimmy. "He'll get that partridge all messed up in no time."

"Would he now?" asked the stranger, lifting his brows in

19

surprise. "Would he be doin' that, now? Well, well, you let him go, and see. I reckon there's a lot more little partridges where the last little old partridge came from."

"Well—" said Jimmy.

And, no matter how interested he might be in talking to the stranger and in finding out from what far-off land he came, he could not help being delighted at a chance to let the big dog perform. It might mean a long chase, eventually, to recapture the brute—but Jimmy pressed the trigger. That is to say, he let go of the chain, and the stiff muscles of big Mishe did the rest. He leaped at the stranger very like a driving bullet, and Jimmy squinted his eyes in joy at the thought of the big man, the partridge, and the dog all inextricably rolled together in the thorny branches of the bush.

He opened his eyes again to see quite another fact.

For Mishe Mukwa had not completed his leap, but on stiffened legs he plowed four furrows in the grass and halted, with frightened hair erect, at the outstretched feet of the stranger.

"He was goin' to scare me," said the latter, in his soft, delightful voice. "Think of that, now. He was goin' to scare poor me!"

And he laughed as he talked, and talked through his laughter in a way which enchanted Jimmy Green more than ever.

"Sit down and rest yourself, puppy," said the other. "Don't you go to upsettin' yourself and me, like that."

He stretched out his hand, and Mishe Mukwa, recoiling, sank on his belly to the ground. There he remained, with his body twitching and his head flattened out between his great forepaws in such a way that every moment Jimmy swore the husky intended to throw his bulk at the throat of the man. Yet it did not happen. Suddenly he saw that Mishe was as thoroughly a frightened dog as ever came under a whip; and that had he been any less mightily courageous, he would have turned and bolted across the meadow.

As it was, he lay at the feet of the man and fought his terror. This troubled Jimmy. It assured him, as his first glance at the stranger had done, that this was indeed a new thing that had walked over the sky line.

Above all, he was amazed at the lack of a pack. The stranger, in the meantime, was stripping the feathers from the partridge, proceeding without haste, but with such skill that a

20

considerable portion of the naked skin appeared at every stroke.

"Your daddy work out at Fort Anxious?" asked the big man, looking up, his fingers seeing their way, unguided.

"I'm Jimmy Green," said the boy. He added in surprise: "I mean, I got no father or mother. I just belong to Fort Anxious."

"Fathers and mothers, they take up a good deal of time," said the stranger.

"Where might you come from, and just what might your name be?" asked Jimmy, almost exploding with curiosity.

"I come from the South," said the other. "I come from the Goldenrod State. The best State in the Union!"

"Is it?" asked Jimmy. "What might make it the best State? Got the most people?"

"No," said the stranger, and paused there, as though this were a sufficient answer. Jimmy went on, busy as a ferret.

"Got the most money?"

"No, Jimmy."

"Just what has it got the most of, then?"

"It's got the most rest," said the stranger. "It's got it in its motto, matter of fact. 'Here we rest.' "

As he ended this sentence, he looked upward to the misty blue of the sky and yawned a little, not offensively, but with such half-closed eyes and with such a sigh that Jimmy suddenly understood why a bear would wish to crawl into a den in the snow and there sleep the long winter sleep.

"Well," said Jimmy Green, "what State might that be, stranger?"

"Alabama, that's my happy home," said the other with an authoritative intonation, very much like that which people use when they are uttering a well-known quotation. "Alabama's where I live. There we rest," said he. "Down there in Alabama! Among the goldenrod, sonny—down there among the goldenrod!"

He yawned again, a mere tightening of the big cords of his neck, together with a smile.

Once more it seemed to Jimmy that this fellow knew something which gave him a tremendous advantage over other men, a mysterious key which opened a door no other man had looked through. He looked from the face of the Alabaman to the quivering body of the Mackenzie husky, and

21

cold awe arose in Jimmy's heart, and a chill of half-frightened pleasure quivered up his spinal column.

"And what might your name be?" asked Jimmy, gently, hardly expecting an answer.

"My name is Joe," said the other.

"Is it? Joe?" said Jimmy Green.

He felt that that name fitted the soft and easy strength and the soft and easy voice of the stranger.

"Joe what?" he ventured.

The smile of the stranger continued, but as he looked at Jimmy the latter had a very new sensation, as though he had walked into a cave and seen eyes in the dark.

CHAPTER FIVE

THIS FEELING did not last long. It switched off and left him, in an odd way, free.

"Joe what?" the man from Alabama was saying.

Still, he did not seem to be looking at his work, but producing a long knife whose blade curved to a fine point, he opened and cleaned the partridge in a moment.

"Joe what?" continued the stranger. "Well, hind names hardly matter a great deal. Smith, Jones, Brown, they jig out of your mind. But they've called me 'Lazy Joe.' I'm not the hardest worker in the world. Never loved a shovel, and never loved a hoe, Jimmy!"

"Oh," said Jimmy.

He could have guessed these things before, and because he felt this truth, he seemed to have been admitted into the inmost and most intimate house of this Southerner's mind.

"Lazy Joe," went on the Alabaman, "by some, and 'Alabama Joe' by a good many more. Alabama Joe I like the best. There's a nice sound to that. It's like something out of a song. You could fit that into a chorus, pretty well, I think.

> "Oh, I miss you so,
> Alabama Joe—"

He sang the words softly, richly, and with a single gesture brought the twang of the banjo into the mind of the boy.

Alabama was smiling again. It was his habitual expression.

"Some people," he went on in his gentle voice, "call me 'Lefty,' because I have two hands."

The boy, with a start, realized that Joe was using the knife with his left hand, though certainly he had shot the partridge while holding the gun in his right. Ambidexterity was something which he had heard of before but never seen.

"Jiminy!" said he. "It's like being two men in one, pretty near!"

"Aye," admitted Joe cheerfully, "and that's a useful thing, because two hands can do just twice as much resting as one. And there are some that call me 'Three-legged Joe,' because I like to use a cane when I'm around a town. A mighty restful thing is a stick, Jimmy."

"Is it?" asked Jimmy, his eyes growing big. "I would figger it just took that much more packin' around!"

"Would you?" said the man from Alabama. "Well, it helps you to stand still, a good deal. Why don't you let your dog have this stuff?"

He had tossed the inwards of the partridge to a little distance, and the boy observed that in all his operations the stranger so scrupulously kept his hands swathed in grass or armed with leaves, that not the least taint of blood appeared upon his finger tips.

"You mean take off the muzzle of Mishe?" asked the boy, astonished.

"Yes."

Jimmy freshened his grip on the big chain.

"He'd take our heads off in two whacks!" said he.

"Would he?" murmured the Alabaman softly. "Would he take our heads off? Eh, boy?"

The wolf dog snarled deep in his throat, but this sound appeared to please Lazy Joe.

"He'll be all right," he said. "If he runs away, I'll catch him for you!"

"You mean, let him go loose?" asked the boy.

"Yeah. I mean that."

"Kite Larkin, he'd skin me alive if I lost that dog!"

"I'll handle that," said Alabama Joe, smiling still, and nodding, and it appeared to young Jimmy that nearly any affair, no matter how important, might safely be left in the hands of such a representative.

Besides, Jimmy took a breathless interest in the testing of

23

this case. Without another word, he removed collar and muzzle by pulling upon a single strap.

Mishe remained flat on his belly, apparently unaware that his great battery of teeth had been unmasked to use as he pleased, while the boy drew back anxiously. He would not have been surprised if Mishe had whirled and flung at him with fangs capable of hamstringing a moose at a stroke.

But for the time being, Mishe remained prone, staring up into the face of Alabama Joe.

"Here," said the latter. "Go get it, boy!"

He extended his hand toward the spoils on the green lawn. Mishe winced but otherwise did not stir.

"There's a proud dog. There's an aristocrat," said Joe. "Look at that, Jimmy! He won't touch food that most dogs would be mighty glad to have."

"You better watch out," cautioned Jimmy. "He's likely to slice your throat open, in about a jiffy! I wouldn't trust him. He's more wolf than he is dog!"

"Ah, no," said Lefty Joe. "Not a wolf! He may look that part, but he has a dog's heart. Craves love, poor boy. Craves petting, too, I dare say!"

At this, he reached out his hand and deliberately laid it upon the muzzle of Mishe, who growled with such terrible fury that his whole body shook.

"Good boy, good boy!" said Lazy Joe carelessly. "He loves petting, you see! Loves it!"

He scratched behind the ears of Mishe, and the snarling of the latter rose to almost a howl of fury, yet he lay as still as though his neck were nailed to the ground.

Jimmy, fascinated, could not believe his eyes.

"I see!" said he. "You're a wild-animal trainer. I've heard of them! You can walk right up and look an elephant in the eye and he gets down and dusts your boots for you!"

"Can I?" smiled Alabama Joe. "Well, it's a new idea to me, Jimmy."

He had broken off a quantity of twigs, by this time, and now he produced a fold of oiled silk from which he took matches. The flame spurted in the cup of his hands. And Mishe, seeing the yellow danger so poisonously near, groaned with heartfelt fear.

Yet still he was turned to stone!

Over the match, the dead twigs sputtered, smoked, and then the fire caught and went crinkling and snapping upward.

More fuel was sprinkled on. Lefty Joe was still talking as he gathered the fire between his hands, molded the flames with his naked touch, as it seemed to the excited mind of the boy.

While that fire waxed—it was very small at the best—Alabama Joe gathered handfuls of the grass and of the budding twigs of the bush, and in this greenery he wrapped the portions into which he cut the partridge. One by one he introduced them to the heart of the fire, piled on more brush, added a large and larger heap, until finally the flames were shooting high, and it seemed to Jimmy Green, as he marveled, that the partridge must have been burned to a crisp, long before.

Yet he knew that it was not.

He began to be willing to venture his very soul that Lefty Joe could not make a serious mistake in this world! What he bade the fire do, that would it do! This, however, and the affair of the partridge, were minor in importance compared with the behavior of the wolf dog.

Fire was the one thing which the husky would hate more than all else. Yet there he lay, with his coat fairly curling and smoking in the heat of the flames, and never once did he strive to rise to his feet, though he had wormed his big body into a sort of half moon to get as far from the heat as possible.

Still he did not rise and bolt.

"Hey!" said Jimmy hoarsely. "What've you done to him? He's gunna be on fire in another minute, I guess!"

"Why, so he is!" exclaimed the Alabaman. "So he is. What's the matter, boy? Are you asleep with your eyes open? Get up, Mishe! Get up, my lad!"

He leaned over the big dog. He snapped his fingers. And at last Mishe Mukwa, leaping sidewise to his feet, bolted with frantic speed out of sight among the pine trees.

CHAPTER SIX

AGAPE, AS HE watched his charge vanish, Jimmy Green lost a little bit of his wonderful respect for the stranger. What would Kite Larkin do? Kite Larkin had a fist as broad as two normal hands, and a pair of shoulders twice as wide as most.

He had sworn that this was the finest Mackenzie husky that ever came out of the Northland, and that, with it, he would be able to break records in the travel over the snow. If Kite did not break him into two pieces for this negligence, it would be very strange.

These thoughts darkened the eyes of Jimmy Green as he looked after his lost husky.

"Well, I reckon that's the end of that dog!"

"Yes, sir," said Happy Joe. "I suppose that's the last time he'll run loose and call himself his own boss!"

"The last time?" said the boy, wondering. "You mean that somebody is going to catch him up again?"

"Of course I do, and you're the somebody," said Alabama Joe. "You've got his collar, haven't you? And I'll bet that you'd be surprised to see how much that big fellow really likes that collar he's been wearing. I'll wager he'd sit up and howl all night for it!"

"Humph!" said Jimmy. "How you gunna catch him?"

"Why, he'll catch himself, son!"

"What!"

"No, I'm betting you!"

"Whacha gunna bet?" asked the boy.

"Anything you want."

Jimmy felt in his pocket. He took out the clouded agate, his prize piece.

"How about that?" he said.

"All right," said the stranger. "The agate against my knife, and I'm betting that before we leave, he'll walk right out of the brush behind us, here."

The mere idea of the great beast crawling and lurking behind that covert made Jimmy squirm most unpleasantly. He cast a glance behind him, and the ghostly wind fled away with a bright footstep over the grass.

"Well," said Jimmy, "I'll take that bet. You mean," he exclaimed, as the enormity of the idea came home to him, "that this same Mishe Mukwa I been working on, will walk out of the brush here and wait for a collar to be put on him?"

"That's what I mean. He'll come along, I'm sure, like a good dog!"

Jimmy drew a great breath. His eyes shone with covetousness, but an honorable soul was stronger still.

"Listen here at me, stranger," said he. "I gotta tell you that that's one of the finest knives that ever I seen, and I could use it, but I wouldn't go snakin' it away from you, anyways, like that. I know something about this here dog, stranger! I'll tell you that!"

"Do you?" asked the Alabaman with much interest.

"You bet your boots that I do! Why, Larkin, he hunted for Mishe two whole years."

"You don't say!"

"Don't I? I do, though! Once he got into a bad storm, freighting up from the lakes, and all at once something hit his team in the front. He thought that it was a lynx gone mad, or a mountain lion, when he got a better look. He jerked out his rifle, but it scooted away. He seen it running, the biggest standing dog he's ever seen, except it looked like a wolf. That was Mishe, and there was two dead dogs in that team."

"Hello!" said Happy Joe. "You don't mean it! Jumped a dog team merely for the fun of it?"

The boy rubbed his knuckles across his chin.

"I'll tell you what," said he. "The fact is that they's a sort of a scar like a collar scar under the fur on one of his shoulders, and that Kite Larkin, he claims that once Mishe was a sled dog, even though he carries his tail low like a wolf!"

"Ah?" said the stranger. "But he caught Mishe at last?"

"Of course he did. Kite, he never would quit a trail. Mishe has cost him three more dogs, and two of 'em leaders! But he trapped him at last. It was a lot of work, though!"

The man from the South smiled on the boy. "Kite gave you that dog to train?" he asked.

"He'd used up his own patience," said the boy, "and there was a pretty good bill from dog breakers, too. So Kite said maybe I wouldn't spoil him, even though I done him no good!"

The Alabaman nodded. "You know dogs, sonny," he suggested.

"Me? Why, I don't know nothin'," said Jimmy. "Not the way that you could handle him—but you was saying that Mishe would come back?"

"I'm betting a knife against that five-clouded agate of yours, Jimmy."

"Well, sir, I reckon that you know your own business—and dogs, better than me. I'll take your bet, then!"

"Sit down," said Lefty Joe. "Sit down and have a leg of the bird with me, will you?"

27

"I've ate," said Jimmy Green. "It wouldn't likely be burned, would it?" he went on, taking a place on the grass near by.

The fire was now scattered. It might have been that Lefty Joe swathed his hands in grass, but certainly he reached into the fire and divided it calmly, and lifted out one by one the four sections of the bird. The smoking, incrusted cinders of the grass in which it had been so thickly wrapped fell away. Then, plucking out a thick, wide leaf, Lefty laid a smoking quarter upon it, and presented it to Jimmy Green.

He did not make it a formal matter, and yet there was a sort of grace and consideration in this gesture that astonished and delighted Jimmy. It was, in some manner, made into an acceptance of him as a full equal.

He was about to refuse this offer. He felt that he must, though the fragrance of the roasted bird rose to his very brain and enwrapped him in excited joy.

"Look here, I've ate," he repeated. "I ain't hungry, and you must be, or you wouldn't've shot so straight."

"I never eat alone," said Alabama Joe.

"Don'tcha?" asked the boy. "Not when you're on the march—all by yourself?"

"You'll find something, if it's no more than a squirrel, or a beetle. It's no luck to eat alone," said the stranger. "Here's to you, Jimmy Green!"

He raised a section of the bird. He smiled behind it. And there was nothing to do but to follow suit.

Jimmy vowed, when he tasted it, that no other partridge ever had flown, like this one, and never before had there been such cookery.

"Supposin' that I hadn't turned up, you'd've had to eat alone, I reckon, Joe?"

"Would I?"

Jimmy looked up into the sky. There was no bird sailing there. He looked down into the grass. Nothing stirred. The wind was still.

"I guess there ain't anything near by," he said, "that would be eating with you?"

"Now, would you bet on that?" asked Lefty Joe, smiling.

"No," said Jimmy hastily, "you bet I wouldn't!"

"All right," went on the Alabaman. "I don't think I'd have far to go to find a pretty healthy appetite to help me out."

He whistled, a thin, shining streak of sound that left a tingle in the ears of Jimmy as it died away.

"Good boy!" said Lefty Joe, and, without turning, he tossed over his shoulder a leg bone of the partridge.

Jimmy observed this act of madness with open mouth, when through the brush just behind Joe, he saw the mighty head and the great shoulders of Mishe Mukwa rising. The bone was snapped from the air by great teeth.

"Jiminy!" said the boy, breathless.

"They'll run in a circle, loose dogs!" said the stranger.

Then, still without looking back, he held another bone over his shoulder. The wolf dog stole forward. With dainty accuracy he picked the bone from the man's fingers with his great white teeth and swallowed it with one champ.

Jimmy scooped the clouded agate from his pocket.

"I reckon this is yours, Joe!" said he, and he held out the marble with both hands.

CHAPTER SEVEN

THEY WALKED DOWN through the bright meadow together. They entered the darkness of the trees, while the boy looked askance at his companion with an increased wonder. Stepping across the even surface of the grass, he never had seen a finer or a freer stride. But once in the forest, Lefty Joe made more noise than a whole tribe of caribou on a stampede!

The boy thought, at first, that it was a joke, and that Alabama Joe was being purposely clumsy in order to make his companion laugh; but after a moment he saw that there was not the slightest wisdom in the feet of the stranger. He did not know how to drop his foot toe first so as to muffle the noise of the impact. He did not know how to roll his weight so that he could pass over twigs without making a sound.

The great man from the South was wasted and lost in the woods. His very way of going was wrong. For he hewed to a straight line, and failed to make those unconscious little deviations of the true woodsman, avoiding half-glimpsed fallen logs, streaks of marsh, soft mud, or thickets where the trunks stand uncomfortably close together. The boy, born to these arts, bred to them, took them almost for granted. And looking up at his new-found friend, he blushed a little. How would Lazy Joe appear in the woods when he stepped out at the side of other men from Fort Anxious?

Even now, however, Jimmy could not merely pity Three-legged Joe. The wolf dog followed at the heels of his accepted master. He kept his nose so close to the hand of the big man that, at every backward swing of that hand, Mishe Mukwa had to shrink and hang a little in his stride. It might be that he was fascinated by hatred, this big dark-coated brute; but Jimmy Green began to suspect that it was something else stirring in the breast of Mishe.

At the outer edge of the woods they paused again, and Alabama Joe looked smilingly down on Fort Anxious, and the gleaming waters of the lake and the bright river.

"Here's a good place," said the stranger.

"It ain't so bad," said Jimmy proudly. "I've heard 'em say, it's about as good a town as they is in the woods."

The other said nothing. He merely stepped a little farther forward and took off his hat so that the strength of the sun could get at him all the better.

"When you was telling me your names," went on Jimmy politely, "you didn't tell me which of 'em you'd prefer that I should call you by."

"They all end one way," pointed out Joe. "So why should I care?"

He went down the slope and into the town, where young Billy Cray saw them almost at once—the stranger and the strange behavior of the big dog. He let out a whoop which raised the boys of the neighborhood as surely as a fire alarm. They came tumbling out and they swarmed around the trio. They accompanied them in state to the shack of Kite Larkin, where Kite himself stood up from whittling a stick into transparent shavings.

Kite waddled about with his chin sunk on his breast in his usual ferocious manner, and saw the dog chained up to the tie post outside his door—saw him actually submit peacefully to the naked hands of the stranger, while his collar and chain were fitted on.

"Well," said Kite Larkin, "I'm danged! Kid, you're a wonder."

"It ain't me!" said the boy in haste. "It's him. It's Alabama Joe. He done it all. You oughta seen it!"

"Yeah?" queried Larkin, eying the stranger up and down. He was not a generous man. There were very few virtues

30

in Kite. But he suddenly dragged out a pair of silver dollars and dropped them into the amazed hands of the youngster.

"I dunno who done the work. I know what the result is, I guess," said he. "And the next time you break a dog for me, kid, you get a higher price still!"

This was a little over twice as much money as ever had been in the possession of young Jimmy Green before. He was fairly tipped sideways by the burden of his treasure. He looked aside at the gently smiling face of big Alabama.

"Joe," said he, "between you and me, you oughta get half this money. You done the training—you done the work, rightly speaking."

"Not me," said the other. "The dog worked himself."

"Come and eat with me," said Jimmy, who could suggest nothing better than this as an entertainment for a grownup.

"What would you do if you were alone?" asked the stranger.

"I'd go over the river and see how the new houses is comin' along."

"Then I'll go along with you. I'd like to see this town, son."

They walked down the street again.

On either side, eyes watched them brightly, covertly as forest animals. And the boy knew that these eyes were noting the holes in the elbows of Alabama's coat, and the lilt of his walk, and the thickness of his shoulders, and the general appearance of tramplike raggedness and good humor. They would write down Alabama very small, he felt; but Jimmy Green almost laughed aloud when he told himself what an awakening they would have.

They turned the first corner—they fairly ran against young Charlie Dyce.

He was hardly to be known by that title any longer, however. He was now Mr. Mounted Policeman Dyce, if you please. He was a member of a picked body. A chosen man for a chosen company!

Mr. Mounted Policeman Dyce caught Jimmy under the pits of his arms and heaved a hundred and twenty pounds high into the air. It was a great feat to toss the equivalent of a wheat sack aloft in this fashion, but the muscles of Charlie Dyce were famous in Fort Anxious.

"Hey, Jimmy!" cried the boy-man. "I'm mighty glad to see you, old son."

31

"Charlie, you ain't in uniform!"

"I've got a vacation."

"For catching those crooks over on Lake Athabasca!"

"I've got a vacation, that's all I know," said Mounted Policeman Dyce. "And this is the first time I ever seen you without a black eye, Jim! What's the matter? Somebody lick the life out of you?"

"Who?" asked Jimmy furiously. Then he laughed. "Charlie," he said, "you never give me no peace, anyway!"

Then he remembered.

"Here's a friend of mine all the way up from Alabama, Charlie. This here is Alabama Joe. This is Charlie Dyce, Joe. He's a mounted policeman!"

They shook hands, and then Charlie Dyce made a quick little back step, as though in haste to get his distance.

"I've seen you before!" he snapped.

It was as plain as plain could be that he did not like Alabama Joe. He had disliked him with one flick of his eyes as heartily as Jimmy had admired the stranger.

Alabama did not answer this remark directly.

"A mounted policeman, as young as that!" said he. "Now, you've got yourself right along in the world, old son, haven't you?"

Charlie did not reply, but he bit his lip. He was very proud, was Charlie.

"I'm mighty glad to know you, Mr. Mounted Policeman Dyce!" said Alabama.

Charlie Dyce flushed. "I've seen you," he repeated.

"In old Mobile," said Alabama.

"Aye, or a thousand mile north," replied Dyce. "I've seen you—"

He paused; his eyes, in the intensity of an effort to remember, wandered far away toward the sky and back again.

"I'll remember," said Dyce, stiffer than ever, and more hostile.

Jimmy flushed a little. He felt that Charlie Dyce was making a great mistake, creating such a scene in the street. He began to edge away, and Alabama went with him.

Then Dyce made a step or two in pursuit and dropped a hand on Jimmy's shoulder.

"This kid is a friend of mine," said Charlie significantly.

"Is he?" answered Alabama Joe. "Well, Dyce, inside and outside of uniform, you're a lucky man!"

CHAPTER EIGHT

ALTHOUGH CHARLIE had turned away behind them, Jimmy still blushed for his old friend.

"Charlie's done a lot," he explained. "He's been wounded and everything. I guess he's as brave as they come, and maybe he's off his feed. Funny—thinkin' that he'd seen you, Joe!"

"Funny, yes," said Alabama Joe.

He reached up and broke a small branch from a tree that grew at the side of the street. Two slashes of his knife turned this many-twigged branch into a straight stick. The knife disappeared. Alabama went on with a new companion. Sometimes he held the improvised cane under his arm, and sometimes he twirled it between his strong fingers like the baton of a bandmaster.

"Maybe Charlie's a little hot-tempered, too," suggested Jimmy, still abased for the conduct of Charlie.

"Why, I didn't notice anything wrong," said Joe. "You take a policeman; to him everybody's guilty till he's proved innocent; and a strange dog is a bad dog, because he's strange. I don't mind. I've been in new towns before, in worse rags than these!"

"He ought to've known!" exploded Jimmy, crimson of face. "He ought to've guessed that you're not—"

"A hobo?" asked Alabama, laughing. "But I am a hobo, old son, when you come to that. Look at my hand!"

He held it out. It was as soft as the hand of a child!

No doubt that was not the whole truth. Otherwise, Alabama would not have mentioned it or shown his hand at all. But Jimmy, though he now wandered in a cloud, began to feel his way dimly toward a light of understanding. There was trouble in the air. No idle thing has made such a man as Alabama Joe walk through the wilderness with, apparently, no greater equipment than a revolver, a knife, and some salt! A man did not walk his shoes to rags and sleep in the cold woods without blankets for nothing. Some very great purpose indeed had made him come all the distance north to Fort Anxious. And young Jimmy Green suddenly would have staked his marbles, his knife, his very rifle, upon the fact that trouble, great trouble, would come to Fort Anxious before it was very much older.

He dared not look squarely at his companion now. At the best, he could use only glances to the side and up, hesitant and uneasy. And then he saw that although Alabama still wore a smile, there was a spot in the center of his cheek which was a little paler than the rest of his face.

He was disturbed. He was very angry, or else—was it possible?—Charlie Dyce had frightened him to the soul. Whether angry or frightened, there was profound darkness ahead! Jimmy sighed as he thought of it. Greatly and rightly he respected the mounted police, but if it came to a contest between their banded forces and the mystery of Three-legged Joe—well, he simply would prefer not to guess the outcome!

They came to the bridge. There Jimmy paused for an instant.

"What's the matter, sonny?" asked Alabama.

"Why, nothin'. But yonder side of the bridge ain't my side. That's all."

"Not your side?"

"My crowd's back yonder. Well, I don't care!"

Alabama said not a word, but he went forward with a lilting, rhythmic sway of the cane, whistling lightly. Yet he made not the slightest reference to the peril which Jimmy was undergoing for his sake.

He knew, but he preferred not to speak of such a thing. It piqued and it interested Jimmy, this attitude. He began to ask himself if the implied challenge of Charlie Dyce might be correct and if his new-found friend was a criminal?

"A fine little ol' town," drawled Alabama.

"Yeah," said Jimmy loyally. "I guess it is, all right!"

"You got some pretty big business up here, too!"

"They get a heap of furs around here," said Jimmy. "You'd be surprised the piles of 'em yonder that come into the big store."

"I bet I would," said Joe. "I've heard of some of the firms. There's Tyndal and Sackett, for instance?"

"Tyndal and Sackett! I bet you'd hear about them! Why, they get most of the lumber money, and they got millions, I've heard folks say. Why, it was their safe that Dillman tried to bust last year."

"Yes?" drawled Alabama.

34

"Tyndal and Sackett, you oughta see their mill up the river."

"Maybe I will."

"A regular mountain of machinery. Old man Tyndal, he's pretty near seventy, now."

"He's got a son, I suppose?"

"Him, no, but there's a fellow by name of Parker that he's the same as adopted. He'll get all of old Tyndal's coin, I suppose."

"He's lucky," said the tramp.

"Well, he's worked for it," declared the boy justly. "Nobody else could've stood the old man the way that that fellow has stood him. That's gunna be his house, over there!"

They stopped at the gate.

"They're gunna have a real lawn, too," said the boy under his breath. "Whacha think about that?"

"He's lucky," repeated the tramp.

"Well, he worked for it," said the boy again. "It's Stanley Parker that killed Bob Dillman."

"Dillman?" said the other. "Dillman? Maybe I've heard of him, somewhere."

"Sure you have. I guess all the papers in the world talked about him! Dillman—he's the fellow that tried to get the money from the Tyndal and Sackett safe. He pretty near did, too. He had it cracked wide open. But Stanley Parker, he walked in and shot it out with the yegg. There ain't any fear in Parker, I guess. He'd fight a grizzly with a knife, most likely."

"This Dillman, he was killed in a fair fight, was he?" asked the man from Alabama.

"Why, of course! The bullet was right from in front. Right between the eyes. That was a fair fight, I guess."

"I've heard of a Bob Dillman," said Alabama, "that was so fast and sure with a gun that he'd knock the cigarette out from between your lips and have his gun put away before you could see who'd fired."

"That's him!" cried the boy. "That's the one. That's why Parker has such a boost, right now. The way he went in there and crashed a man like that Dillman! Well, I wouldn't've had the nerve."

"No?" said the tramp politely.

"Parker, he goes down the street. He sees a wink of light behind the window at the side of the lumber office. Just a

35

...k. That was all. Well, he took a long look. There wasn't another glimmer. It might've been a reflection in the glass, he says to himself, but he ain't the sort that would let anything go by him without takin' a look at it! Not him! He didn't go for help, either."

"He went in to take a look, did he?" asked the tramp.

"That's just what he done. Slipped in soft, not makin' no noise—"

"This Bob Dillman that I've heard about," said the tramp carelessly, "was a fellow who could hear a mouse twitchin' his whiskers in the dark."

"Yeah?" asked the boy. "Well, he didn't hear Stanley Parker."

"It seems he didn't!" said the tramp, with an odd intonation.

But when the boy looked sharply up at him, Alabama Joe was smiling at a magpie which had flashed across from tree to tree.

"He didn't hear a thing," insisted the boy. "He just found himself facing Stanley Parker."

"Did he?"

"Yes. And mind, Parker, he didn't have a gun!"

"Ah?" says the tramp.

"But Parker, he didn't have any fear. He just sings out and tells Dillman to surrender."

"But he wouldn't?"

"No, he went for his gun; and Parker, he rushed in and they had a struggle. Jiminy! I would've liked to seen that, if I wasn't too scared to look."

"This Bob Dillman that I've heard of was a great wrestler," said the tramp idly.

"Was he? Well, Parker's strong as a bull. You never seen such a man. He took the gun right away from Dillman. Dillman pulled a knife. Parker had to shoot him, and he done a good job, right between the eyes!"

The tramp, to the amazement of Jimmy, began to whistle.

"Hey, Joe, don't you b'lieve what I'm tellin' you?"

"Believe you?" said the other absently. "Of course, I believe you. I was just thinking."

"Thinking of what?"

"Just thinking what a really cool hand that Parker must be—to pick out the head instead of the body. With a fellow

36

like that Bob Dillman rushing in at him! That was all I was thinking about. Is this the end of the town?"

"No, there's the old mill and—"

"Well, I've seen enough. Suppose we ramble back?"

CHAPTER NINE

THEY TURNED BACK toward the river.

The mind of Alabama Joe seemed to cling to the story of Bob Dillman.

"I suppose that this Parker's a great shot and hunter around here, sonny?" said he.

"Parker? Well, he's too much business to bother with hunting. Nobody knew he was such a great fighter with guns. Not till it come to the killing of Dillman. Fists—yeah! He always could tie the lumberjacks in knots, and they ain't exactly limber like string! But guns, he showed what he could do when the pinch come. I guess they ain't a man in Fort Anxious that would like to look crooked at Stanley Parker. Would you?"

He grinned aside at the big man, and Lazy Joe instantly held up a protesting hand.

"I'm the most peaceablest man that ever come to this town," he assured the boy. "I'd walk a hundred mile to keep away from trouble—if I had the shoes to do it in! So Stanley Parker, he never was much of a hunter?"

"No. He never bothered."

"I suppose he was always around practicing with revolvers, though?"

"Not so's anybody could've noticed it. No, that wasn't his way at all. Some folks," pondered Jimmy Green, "are just nacherally born able to do things, I guess!"

"Yeah," admitted Alabama. "But I've heard of gun fighters that had a good deal of natural talent, which they kept cultivated like a melon patch. Two hours a day, loading, firing, snap shots, beads, shooting on the turn, lying down, to the side, over the shoulder, under the arm, off a horse galloping, trotting, walking, falling to the ground, sitting, jumping up, to the side. I never yet met a good one that didn't need that sort of practice. That Bob Dillman, I've heard them say, was

37

a fellow that would rather have a toothache than go without gun practice every day of his life. But you see what it all came to!"

He made a gesture with his empty hand, keeping the stick under the pit of his arm.

"He must've been a pretty important man," suggested the boy. "Dillman, I mean."

"From what I've heard, I guess that he was. They raise their girls few but pretty up here, sonny. That's the way with most good crops."

She had just turned the corner with big Stanley Parker at her side. And though the heart of Jimmy was stabbed with jealousy, he had to admit that they made a fine pair together.

"That's the finest girl in town. She ain't a crop. She's all alone!" said Jimmy. "That's the grocer's daughter. That's Paula Carson." He looked up to Alabama Joe. "You wanta meet her, Joe, I guess?"

"Of course I do," said Alabama Joe.

It seemed as though Parker would have gone by, even though Jimmy patently had halted to speak, but Paula Carson paused. Parker stopped impatiently. Proudly the boy introduced his companion. What were ragged coats, in his eyes?

"Here's a pretty good friend of mine, Paula Carson. This is Alabama Joe. And here's Mr. Stanley Parker, Joe. This is the man that done for Bob Dillman!"

Paula Carson shook hands. Mr. Parker did not. He was a very big young man, a little white and pink from indoor work, but with a great arch to his chest, and a grand hang to his shoulders.

"Been a long time on the road coming up here, Alabama?" he asked indifferently.

"Yeah," said Alabama in his soft voice, with his usual smile. "Not so many doors to batter, most of the way. Mighty glad to meet the man that did up Bob Dillman."

"Did you know him?"

"He ran me out of a saloon, one day."

"Oh," said the boy. "That's why you know about him, Joe?"

"Sure," said Alabama. "He was pretty hard, that fellow Dillman."

"We're apt to have a harder one up here," said Parker—he spoke to the girl, not to the others.

"What do you mean, Stanley?"

"Kill one snake and its mate turns up. Dillman's partner is likely to show up one of these days."

"But not as bad a man as Dillman, I suppose?"

"Not as bad!" exclaimed the other. "Why, Paula, Dillman's partner was the Stingaree!"

"Stingaree?" she murmured. "I've heard of that name, I think! I thought it was a horrible ray that lay in the sand and the sun, with a sting ready to whip into you!"

"That's what a stingaree is," said Parker. "But *the* Stingaree is a man. He's twice a Dillman, they tell me."

"Who told you, Stanley?"

"Charlie Dyce. He's full of the Stingaree! He spent an hour warning me, and gave me a spring holster to carry my gun." He looked up the street impatiently. "We'd better go on, Paula. If we're to have time to look over the house."

She seemed hardly to hear. She was looking straight and hard at the stranger.

"You're a new friend to Jimmy?" she asked.

"Jimmy's showing me the town," he nodded.

"No one knows it half so well," said she. "Jimmy, take care of yourself!"

She went off beside Parker, with a smile, leaving Jimmy to wonder if there was something of a hidden meaning in her last speech. He stared after her with a sigh.

"I might've guessed that it would be Parker, one of these days," said Jimmy. "Suppose he wants her?"

"Why, he'd have her, I suppose," said Alabama Joe. "He looks like a fellow who gets his own way."

"He's never lost yet," sighed Jimmy. "And she—"

He swallowed his misery. Another thought flashed across his mind.

"That man they call the Stingaree. Suppose he should come up here, Alabama?"

"The Stingaree?" said the other slowly. "I don't know that I've ever seen him. Heard of him, maybe. The name sort of sticks in my mind. Hello, Jimmy! Look at this! Mishe Mukwa got lonely, I suppose."

Around the corner, came the great wolf dog. He came hard and fast, head and tail stretched in a line, but when he saw the two, he doubled in back of them and ran straight up behind Alabama Joe.

"Joe!" shouted the boy. "Look at there! He's come to you! He's your dog, Joe!"

39

"Kite Larkin won't agree to that, I suppose," said the tramp cheerfully. "He looks pretty hot."

They had crossed the bridge, and Kite Larkin hove in view, running at full speed, with a rawhide rope in one hand and a whip in the other. He came up sputtering curses.

"You doped that dog for the kid, and now you've tried to steal him!" he yelled at the tramp. "I'm gunna bash your face in for you, dang you!"

"Hold on, hold on!" said Alabama Joe, as softly as ever. "I don't want any trouble, Larkin!"

"I'll bust your jaw for you!" said Larkin, and smote with all his might.

Alabama Joe shrank back, and the heavy fist drove past his head. Larkin floundered with the heaviness of his effort. As for poor Jimmy Green, his heart turned cold. He wanted to cover his eyes to shut out this scene of horror. But he could not.

He was forced to stand by, and see his great champion from the Southland show the white feather in the most shameful way.

Kite Larkin was only the more furious because he had failed in his first attempt. He swerved about again and charged bellowing, head down. He was built like a bull. Like a bull he fought, hungry to close in and gore. Alabama Joe had barely time to dodge. It was a very close thing between his ducking head and the crashing fist of Kite. But the latter, lunging on, struck the leg of Alabama with his lifting knee, and spilled heavily over it.

Too heavily! Up through the dust of the street there appeared the hard, polished knuckle of a root and against this Kite rapped his head so roundly that he quivered, and lay still.

"There, there," said Alabama. "I didn't want any trouble. That's hard luck. He'll murder me for this, Jimmy! Here, we'd better take him away and get some water—"

He lifted the inert bulk of Larkin in his arms, raising it so easily that Jimmy Green forgot to wonder at the strength his friend had showed. Besides, Jimmy was too filled with shame for the cowardice of Alabama, too sick and hurt with disgust.

He saw the tramp carrying Larkin across the street, and trailed along miserably, only grateful that there had been no spectators. The front of the Carson grocery store blinked its windows behind the trees. Into that cool and fragrant place the tramp carried his burden and laid Larkin on the long counter.

Old Carson himself was there, of course, his white hair looking whiter and his red face looking redder than usual.

"You'd better get out of here," he said to the tramp, when the trouble had been explained. "Larkin'll murder you for this."

"That's why I'm going to stay where I have witnesses and friends," said Alabama. "I'm not a fighting man, Mr. Carson."

"Ain't you?" asked Mr. Carson, staring at the stranger with lips that began to curl. "You don't fight?"

"No," said the tramp, "and I'm too short-winded to run. So you can see the fix that I'm in. I'll stay right here till he wakes up, and then I'll apologize."

CHAPTER TEN

IT SEEMED IMPOSSIBLE to Jimmy Green, this melting away of his hero to a normal figure of failing humanity. He could not believe that the great man was fallen. For his own part, he could not talk. He remained in the background.

It was a long time before Kite Larkin regained consciousness. He lay utterly relaxed, almost like death. Jimmy Green was afraid that the thick neck of Kite had been broken, but Carson had no such fears. He simply said:

"He'll wake up with a jump and start smashin' things. That's his style! That dog of his has given him a taste of tooth, eh?"

Kite was wearing a coat of heavy leather, and this was laid open from the point of the shoulder to the small of the back in one enormous slash.

"A little higher and that jump would have reached the neck," pointed out Carson.

Just at this moment Kite Larkin sat up with a grunt, rolled his eyes, and then hurriedly jumped down from the counter.

He saw big Alabama Joe and went for him with a yell, while Alabama got behind a towering barrel. The grocery-man picked up a sawed-off shotgun from behind his counter.

"Kite!" he bellowed. "Get out of here! I ain't going to have you mess up my nice clean floor, for me. Get out of here!"

Kite Larkin stopped. He rocked forward on his tiptoes and almost overbalanced in the struggle between desire to get at his enemy and reluctance to move the trigger finger of Carson.

He compromised by cursing Alabama Joe in a furious outburst.

"Are you gunna stand there and take that?" asked Carson in deep contempt. "You're his weight and mor'n his height!"

"I'm a peaceful man," said Alabama undisturbed. "I don't want trouble with any man, Carson."

"I'll come back and get you with a gun!" shouted Kite. "I'll come back and get your scalp!"

"You spill a drop of blood on my floor and I'll make you take it out ag'in with your teeth!" declared Carson. "Get out of here, and take your dang dog with you!"

"He ain't my dog," answered Kite, more incensed than ever. "He ain't half of my dog. He's been doped and hypnotized by that limber-jointed yaller hound yonder, and stole into the bargain."

"He ain't stolen," said Carson. "There he stands for you to take!"

"He nigh had my throat before," said Kite. "I'm comin' back with a gun to get Mishe and the yellow loafer that you call a friend, Bill Carson!"

"No man that won't fight is a friend of mine," stated Carson. "But I'll tell you this: Bloodshed—man or dog—in my house, and I'll slaughter the gunman that sheds it. You hear me, Larkin?"

"I'll get you, too!" yelled Larkin, gone frantic at this opposition. "I'll end the three of you. It's a dang plot!"

He rushed out the door and went up the street at full speed, waving his arms. Bill Carson looked after him with a scowl and an apprehensive shake of his head.

"He means what he says!" he declared. "Jimmy, Charlie Dyce is back in town. You go and tell him to head off that wrong-headed fool of a Larkin. Hurry up, Jimmy, or all the soap and the water in the world won't wash this floor again!"

Jimmy gave one sad glance at Alabama Joe. The latter had remained behind the barrel, and the only comfort which Jimmy gained was that at least his man of mystery had not changed color or so much as lost his habitual lazy smile.

With all his might, Jimmy bolted up the street and found Charlie Dyce where he expected that hero to be, that is to say, leaning over the fence of the Hudson house and grinning foolishly and happily as he chatted with Minnie Hudson.

Wildly came Jimmy and jerked at Charlie's arm.

"Charlie, Charlie!" he called frantically. "Will you come and stop Kite Larkin?"

"What's Kite up to?" asked Charlie Dyce. "Besides, I'm not on duty, Jimmy, now. I'm off on a vacation."

"Charlie, he's gunna do a murder! He's gone for his gun!" shouted the boy.

"Is he?" snapped Charlie Dyce.

He turned on his heel and jerked his hat over his eyes.

"Who's he after?" he demanded quickly, stepping out beside the boy.

"He's after Alabama Joe—"

Mounted Policeman Dyce halted in mid-stride with rather a disgusted look.

"The tramp?" he said.

"He's gunna be murdered!" said Jimmy, dancing and almost screaming in his anxiety. "And he's the best dog-trainer in the world—and he won't fight—and he's gunna be murdered!"

"That hobo's the best dog-trainer in the world, and he won't fight—and he's going to be murdered, is he?" asked Charlie Dyce, in strangely sour mockery. "Lemme tell you, son, that he won't be murdered. Not by three Kites, put all together. Now you run along and keep your hat on!"

With this statement, he turned back to his fence, and eased his hat on his head again, while Jimmy remained aghast.

"It's time Kite had a lesson, anyway," said Charlie Dyce over his shoulder.

This completed the stupefaction of Jimmy Green. Charlie Dyce had acted as though Alabama Joe was a tower of strength, and Kite Larkin, that formidable warrior, a mere foolish child.

Jimmy went on, bewildered.

He thought back upon the scene which he had just witnessed in the street and in the grocery store. Then, glancing back, he saw Kite lurching along at a great rate, his face set, a rifle swinging in his hand. He went past Charlie at the Hudson's place, or almost past him, when Charlie turned and

43

tapped Kite on the shoulder. The dog-freighter whirled about in high excitement.

All that Jimmy could see was that Dyce hooked a thumb over his shoulder in the direction of the Carson grocery store. He could not have had time to say more than a half dozen words, but to the utter amazement of the boy, Mr. Larkin turned about and went off, very much like one who has been under the whip.

It was another poser for Jimmy Green.

He would have given his two dollars to know what had been spoken by Charlie Dyce. But, doubtless, he had threatened Kite with the wrath of the mounted police unless he returned peaceably to his home. There could be no other reasonable explanation, and yet the boy still had an idea that this might not be all.

He went back to the grocery store in this haze of doubt, and looking inside, he saw his big Alabama friend perched on the top of the great barrel, sitting on his hands, and chewing a straw pulled out of one of the brooms which stood near by.

"Why not?" Alabama was asking.

"Why so?" thundered Bill Carson, who seemed to have been greatly irritated by something in this talk.

"Why not?" echoed Alabama Joe.

"A dog-gone fellow that won't fight his own fights!" exploded Carson. "I don't wancha around. You'd be in here crawlin' around behind my leather skirts, for one thing! It ain't my way to hurt a man's feelings, but you've asked for it!"

"Some men are born brave, and some are educated to it, and some grow brave in time and with good examples," said Alabama Joe. "Now, with a good example like you in front of me, you can't tell, Mr. Carson. I might turn into a regular stick of dynamite."

"A man your size!" grunted Carson. "And afraid to hold your head up and call your soul your own!"

"I'll learn from you, Mr. Carson. One steady old horse in every span, that's what makes the wagon go."

"You got some sense," said the other, "but a lot of good you'd do for me, with your elbows sticking out of your sleeves and your toes sticking out of your boots!"

"I'll buy slippers," said Alabama. "They have a good soft sound, and I won't wear a coat. I'll use an apron instead.

Look me over, Mr. Carson. 'Always polite' is my motto. I might do you a lot of good behind that counter, if you'll give me a chance. That is, unless there's a lot of heavy lifting."

"Young man," said Carson, glaring beneath his bent brows, "are you by any chance kidding me?"

"Me?" asked Alabama, raising his head with an expression of the utmost innocence. "I'm asking for a job, Mr. Carson! There's the dog, too, you know."

Carson turned purple.

"What danged good will a dog do me, I'd like to know?" he roared. "A wolf of a brute like that, ready to take off legs at the hip and arms at the shoulder?"

"Well," said Alabama, "for one thing, everybody in Fort Anxious is going to drop in to see a hundred-and-sixty-pound Mackenzie husky that's been trained by mesmerism! Am I wrong?"

"Listen to me," answered the grocer. "I'd ought to throw you out in the street. But I ain't going to. You've got ideas enough to run a railroad. I can use you in here, and between us, we'll put Maker and Webb out of business. When can you go to work?"

"I'm working now!" said the tramp.

CHAPTER ELEVEN

No one affair can hold all the attention of a king who has a mind as wide as his realm; Jimmy Green slipped away from the grocery store, called by business. Rumor had it that the Eastsiders—they were the crew on the farther side of the river—had enlisted a most desirable addition. He was a Cree boy, belonging to a family which recently had come to town. Since his clothes were certainly the least of his burdens, the boys of Fort Anxious had been able to view with much interest a wide and muscular pair of shoulders. He walked, moreover, like a cat on wet ground. He made less sound than a shadow and raised no dust at all. This fellow had joined the enemy forces, and it had been a bitterly begrudged addition on the part of Jimmy. On this day, for the first time, Cracking Thunder, which was the gentle name of the new lad, was to be seen at the pool.

It was neutral ground. There the rival bands met to compare bruises, and make boasts, and parade victories. It was neutral ground because though there was water all around the town, most of it was as cold as ice, whereas from the first long spring day the water of the pool was deliciously mild. Both factions had vowed that they must enjoy it in peace.

So there went Jimmy, the king, to see the enemy knight in action. He arrived just in time to see the young Cree balanced on a branch that thrust out fully thirty feet above the surface of the water. It was a dizzy height. The branch, moreover, was dead, and one could hear ominous creakings as the weight of the stranger rested upon it. Yet Cracking Thunder stood easily erect, his arms folded, looking over the sky, the water, and the gaping boys around the shore.

"Is he gunna jump off of that?" asked Jimmy Green, in an anguish of terror and admiration.

"Shut up," said his clansman. "Sure he is. Look it!"

"I, Cracking Thunder," said the boy in Cree, which was perfectly well understood by nearly all the white lads, "shall dive into this water. The water is not very deep. But I shall not break my neck. The Under Water People are my friends. They assist me."

"He's a blow-hard," said Jimmy fiercely. "He's talked so much, he won't do nothing!"

He was doomed to disappointment.

At that very moment the young Cree leaned forward into the air and fell like a copper bolt, gathering such speed that it was a glance of light rather than a body that slid into the water of the pond.

Every boy rose to see. Every boy gaped with awe.

Behold! the water leaped and plopped loudly behind the heels of Cracking Thunder.

"Where is he?" shouted someone.

"I see him! He's stickin' feet up in the mud!"

"He's broke his neck!"

"Somebody help!"

"Hey," screamed the youngest boy of all. "Look!"

He was too young to be noticed, but there was something in his voice at this moment that pulled eyes his way, and following the direction in which he was pointing, they saw with utter amazement that in the midst of their excitement Cracking Thunder had risen from the water and now was sitting in

46

the mossy arm of a big, crooked root that protruded from the bank.

He was calmly wringing the water from his long hair as though these mundane affairs were of no interest to him.

But from the boys there went up such a prolonged racket that it was like the applause which welcomes a famous actor. They yelled, they whooped. They turned handsprings.

The king waited.

He was sick at heart. He knew that his turn would soon come. He knew when eyes would turn toward him. The king must excel all with fist, and wrestling, and at the gun. He must run fast enough to catch the long-distance runner, and far enough to outwind the sprinter. Besides, in all things he must rival every lad, no matter what a genius he might be.

Therefore, Jimmy knew what to expect.

All eyes flashed toward him. He heard voices that seemed to his dizzy ears wailing from a great distance: "Come on, Jimmy!"

Jimmy came on.

He felt that he was going to die. But he advanced to the old tree and went up its gnarled trunk. Past the first branch, from which they all dived, though some of the younger boys were afraid even of this. Past the second, from which he, on one or two grand occasions, had plunged into the water. Past the third he went, from which no boy had yet dared to drop. To the fourth, still loftier, he climbed. But still he was not at the branch from which the Cree had dived.

He had to go up, and up. And at last he had reached the summit of the lightning-broken and blasted tree. He stood there grappling the splintered top of the trunk, his feet on the rain-eaten rotten bough on which the Cree boy had stood as on a stage. And, looking down, he saw strained, excited faces looking up at him.

"I can't do it!" said Jimmy to his heart.

A dead hush made him look—a dead hush, broken by insulting laughter.

He stared down. It was Cracking Thunder who pointed a coppery, sleek arm up at him and laughed with savage joy to see the white boy cling to the tree trunk.

"I'm gunna die," said Jimmy to himself. "I can't do it."

He thought of pretty Paula Carson. Her face had been the stimulant which had driven him, like a gallant knight, many a time back into the battle to make the final and the

47

decisive charge. But she was a haze in his mind at this moment. Then he thought of the tramp, not, strange to say, as he had shrunk behind the barrel away from the fury of Kite Larkin, but as he had stood in the meadow, with the partridge dead on the grass, and a wisp of gun smoke streaked in the air before him—Alabama Joe, smiling, easy.

"I can't do it!" said Jimmy Green.

He set his teeth. His nostrils flared. He made one quick step and leaped from the breaking bough into the naked air.

Under him the flat face of the pool extended hard as sheet steel and the same color. He drew in his stomach and stiffened his legs with a quiver. He was rushing down.

Then, unbelievably hard, his hands struck the surface of the water and his elbows buckled. He felt the *whack* of the stinging water on his stomach. He felt it beat like a club against his legs, and then he was rushing at a headlong speed.

The grisly head of a submerged trunk reached at him like a living danger. A fish winked out of his path. He was hurt, he was half stunned. He could not tell whether or not his body had been split open like a fish by the cleaner's knife.

And then it seemed to him that he could not hold his breath longer. He remembered to strike out with hands and feet, and suddenly his head popped out of the water.

What shouting! His clansmen danced in an ecstasy. Even the foes shouted and whirled their arms above their heads, for, in a way, this was a vindication of Fort Anxious against the outer world.

No matter that he had crashed into the water like a stone. What was of importance was that he had accomplished the dive, without practice, at the very first challenge. That was what deified him in the eyes of his confederates.

He swam, and floated lazily on his back.

"How was it? Hey, Jimmy, how was it? Get hurt?"

"Aw, that ain't anything!" said Jimmy. "Go on, Cracking Thunder, and try it again. Go on, Cracking Thunder!"

"Go on, try again, Cracking Thunder," yelled the united voice of both clans.

But Cracking Thunder did not stir. He was simply staring, agape, at the dead bough, for the thrust of Jimmy's feet had brushed it down, and it hung by a veritable thread! So much for Cracking Thunder and so much for all challengers! The king still lived!

48

CHAPTER TWELVE

THE DIZZY MIND of the boy cleared gradually. He was not only sure of his victory and the subduing of Cracking Thunder, but he also was able to reflect a little upon the oddities of the strange world. For his own part, he knew very well that chance had played two thirds of the part in keeping him from crashing with a flat body upon the stinging surface of the water. Even as it was, he had gone in with a great awkward splashing, not at all to be compared with the snaky smoothness and the ease of the Indian. However, this would not be counted against him, and he would never again be called upon to display his skill as a high diver. He simply had established himself once more as a boy who would do anything that any other boy dared!

Then he swam to the shore and sat upon the bank, drying out by degrees, resting on his laurels.

The sun dropped lower. The smaller boys went shivering home. At last, Jimmy stepped into his rags and left the woods. It was the red gold of the sunset when he came down the street through the town. Jimmy was a little tired, mentally, spiritually, and in body. The hollowness inside him seemed to reach from his chin to his toes, and enchanting savors of cookery were in the air.

He cast about in his mind as to where he should dine.

He had money in his pocket, now. He could go into the hotel dining room, if he chose, and eat among the men there. But since Kite Larkin had lost his dog, he might ask for his money back. Jimmy sighed and delayed judgment on those two broad, heavy dollars. Perhaps they still were not his. In the meantime, there were twenty tables where he would be expected if he cared to show himself.

He felt no shame to accept charity, for charity, to be sure, it was not. He helped at the winter traps, the winter freighting. He knew how a skin was fitted on a beaver or a marten as well as any man, and was just as fast and expert at taking it off. Or, for that matter, he could hunt for the pot and fill it as well as most of the good shots in the village. And those rubber-tough strings of muscles across his shoulders and back had been built up by steady swinging of an ax, turning logs and branches into convenient lengths for stove and fireplace. He never received money for this work. Sometimes he got a bit of cast-off clothing; but, on the whole, he was expected to pay himself by dropping in for meals whenever he chose. He was always welcome, not only because he knew how to work, but also because he was sort of unofficial newspaper. He knew every bit of gossip, every quarrel, every reconciliation, every arrival, every departure. For all these reasons, Jimmy could cast about him and choose where he would.

When he passed the house of the Widow Duval, he paused, and his nose quivered like the nostrils of a rabbit. There was no doubt about it. She was making what in other hands became a stew; but Madame Duval turned it into a savory delicacy. Jimmy knew where he would dine that night! Besides, had he not half-filled her woodshed for the preceding winter?

His attention was called ahead, just at this moment, to a thick circle of people in the very center of the street. There were men, women, children. There were some on horseback. Others had drawn up in buggies and stood up to stare at some great attraction in the center of the circle, so Jimmy trotted up.

He heard laughter, then shouts of applause as he came nearer. So he made himself smaller, and dodging, ducking, twisting, sliding, he got close to the innermost rim of the spectators. What he saw inside made his heart sink.

It was Alabama Joe, juggling, with his hat upon the ground before him! Yes, juggling like a beggar to raise money. The bottom of that old felt hat now glistened with a silver gilding, and every now and then a fresh shower of quarters, and dimes, and even half-dollars clinked into it. Making money fast—just like a beggar!

Jimmy Green was the most loyal soul in the world, but this was a little too much for him. He looked back from the performer, wondering why there was such an open space in that direction, and he saw that here lay Mishe Mukwa in the dust of the street, lolling out his long red tongue, and smiling up at his new-found master so broadly that his eyes almost disappeared.

Alabama Joe was juggling knives. He had five of them in the air. He handled them as though they were water and his hands the nozzles of two hoses. He showered the bright steel high, he let it dwindle and bubble low. Sometimes the stream poured over his shoulder and around under his lifted leg. Sometimes the heavy hunting knives seemed to be walking with great strides up the center of his back, and toppling off with a stagger from his forehead to fall into the ready hands again.

"Mr. Chalmers!" said the tramp, as the applause roared.

And he hurled one of the knives so that it entered the grounds with a thud and struck there buried to the hilt exactly between the narrowly separated toes of Spud Chalmers.

"Monsieur Piombleu!"

At the feet of the startled Canuck fell another knife.

Swift the four knives flashed out and returned each to its original owner. The fifth disappeared—melted from the hands of the wizard.

"But my own knife, ladies—gentlemen!" said the tramp. "I had it here. Did some one pick it out of the air by mistake? Sorry! I'll have to look around among you unless somebody'll speak up and admit that he has it. Speak up, please!"

Instead of answering, all looked around with delighted grins.

"I've got to search you, then," said the tramp. "Don't like to do this. Excuse me, everybody—"

He was circling slowly before them, and the great dog like a shadow stalked at his heels.

At last, the entertainer came before Madame Dugommier. She had her mouth open, grinning, her hands folded beneath her apron and across her fat stomach. She was teetering back and forth in purest enjoyment of this free show. For certainly a Dugommier would never contribute—not even to pay an honest bill!

The juggler paused in front of her.

"Madame, terribly surprised—a woman of your standing—leading lady—social reputation. Madame, I beg your pardon, but I certainly need that knife."

He reached out. From the hair—no, it was the ear of Madame Dugommier that gave up the knife.

He seemed to have difficulty. He seemed to be tugging, still apologizing for making so free with her.

Out came the knife.

"Madame, in your ear! If only I had failed to see the tip of the handle there, with my initials carved on it, I never should have guessed—but in the ear! What wonderful ears, Madame Dugommier! What extraordinary ears! It would take a thick

51

wall and a whisper to keep madame from hearing, I suppose!"

The whole crowd yelled with delight, for she was a known and prying gossip. Madame Dugommier clapped her hands to her head.

"My ear!" she screamed, and fled through the crowd for her house as fast as she could scamper.

From nearly every hand flashed a bit of bright metal. There was a constant clinking of the silver as it rained into the hat of Alabama Joe.

He picked up the hat. He made a little speech. He thanked them. He thanked the entire town of Fort Anxious, and would be very glad to receive them—he and Mishe Mukwa —at any time they cared to drop in at the Carson grocery store, whose goods, besides, were three times better and cheaper than those of Maker and Webb. For his own part, he, Alabama Joe, was so enchanted with Fort Anxious that he expected to stay there the rest of his life. Their money looked so good to him that he could eat it—without a sauce!

Behold! He tilted his hat at his lips. He opened his mouth wide. The tide of silver coins flowed into it. Yes, the money could be seen and heard chattering musically against his teeth.

He finished. The hat was empty. He showed its emptiness. Then he groaned a little and placed his hand upon his stomach.

"Even good silver is a little indigestible!" said he. "But if my stomach doesn't want to be my purse, it doesn't have to be. Come, then, I'll take the money back! Ah, here it comes!"

Right down out of his sleeve it poured. He had to shake his arm vigorously to dislodge it, but out came the pieces, pouring heavily down into his coat pocket, while Fort Anxious shook with enjoyment.

But Jimmy Green drew mournfully back into the outer shadows.

A coward—well, that was an affliction sent from heaven. But a begging charlatan and public entertainer—that was too bad! He turned on his heel and started for Madame Duval's table.

CHAPTER THIRTEEN

THAT NIGHT all went well at Madame Duval's. The ragout was what Jimmy's soul desired, and the only trouble was that after the meal, after the dishes had been done up, he had to sit for a time and listen to Madame Duval pump at a little organ with all her might while she screeched out old French songs. But his adventures for that night were not yet over. There was a knock at the front door, and Jimmy himself opened it upon the fine face of young Charlie Dyce. Charlie wanted him. He left at once.

In the outer dark, he walked slowly on with Charlie, proud of such company. Charlie was very friendly and confidential.

"That big bum that you met today in the woods, Jimmy," said the mounted policeman, "what did he tell you about himself?"

"That he came from Alabama," said the boy.

"Well," said Dyce surprisingly, "he didn't. What else did he tell you?"

"Nothing," said Jimmy. "Now I come to think of it, he talked right along, but he never said much about himself. Why d'you call him a bum, Charlie?"

"Say, Jimmy, it's pretty plain that he is. A crook!"

"I dunno," said Jimmy. "He was pretty white to me. He's about the best dog-trainer in the world, I guess." Then he added bitterly: "And juggler, too!"

"He can train dogs, and he can juggle," admitted Dyce earnestly, "but that's not all he can do, and that's why I want you to help me, Jimmy."

"Help you to do what?" asked Jimmy, amazed to find Charlie Dyce leaning upon him.

"You can do what nobody else can," replied Dyce. "You're a big chief in this here Fort Anxious, Jim. You can put twenty sharp scouts on a trail and follow it till it fades into the air. I want you to trail that Alabama Joe."

"Why?" asked Jimmy sharply.

"I dunno," said Charlie Dyce, with a sigh. "If I knew why I wanted to trail him, exactly, I probably wouldn't have to ask you at all."

53

He paused. "I could put the irons on him and take him for a ride to prison!"

There was a little click of the teeth of Dyce—as though he were fitting the handcuffs upon big Alabama Joe that very instant.

Jimmy drew a great breath.

"He couldn't be very much," said he. "Look what a coward he is! Not ashamed to show it, in front of everybody!"

"Listen, Jim! I'd rather tackle ten Kite Larkins than one Alabama Joe. You hear?"

"Of course I hear," said Jimmy. "You don't mean it, Charlie?"

"Here I am, saying it. I want you to help me, Jimmy. I'm trying to find out who he is. But I doubt that I'll have time. It means waiting for mail, and telegraph on top of the mail, and even joining the two together, it will take days and days. In the meantime, what's he come here to Fort Anxious for?" He snapped his fingers. "You see, Jim, I'm telling you things that you'll never breathe to a soul?"

"I'll be dumb as a dog-gone stone," said Jimmy honestly.

"When I think of it, it makes me excited. I'll be raised. I'll be boosted," Charlie said softly to himself, "if I can land this fish. What's brought him up here? Overland—marching himself ragged—going through torture!"

"He's fat," said Jimmy hopefully. "He didn't walk that off."

"He could get fat on cactus gristle if he wanted to," said the mounted policeman, filled with his business. "But the fat doesn't talk. What really counts is that he's come without a pack, without a horse—why. I'll bet you that he's hardly marched twenty miles in his life before. Railroad cushions and a Mexican saddle, they've done his legging for him!"

"I thought he was only a tramp," said Jimmy.

"Sure he is. A tramp. A tramp royal, that's what he is, and what he's got up his sleeve is the thing that I want to know. He'd never come here for a little thing. Money or revenge—one of the two! Jim, will you help me out?"

It was the greatest temptation Jimmy ever had endured in his young life. He bit his lips and sighed.

"Charlie," said he, "it would be fine to do something for you and with you. But you take this Alabama Joe—I was the first fellow he met from Fort Anxious—he broke that dog for me—he made me two dollars—"

54

"I'll give you twenty if you can give me any real information. Shadowing him, for me, would be a hard thing to do. But kids like you and your gang, he never would be able to suspect you! You'd put him in a glass case!"

Charlie Dyce fairly panted with earnestness, but the boy answered slowly:

"I mean, that him and me, we sat down and we ate something. It was his meat that I bit onto, Charlie. I guess that it would be double-crossing him to go agin' him now."

There was a faint groan from the other.

"Jim! You're a friend of his?"

"I have to call myself that," said Jimmy.

"Well, let it go. Dang it if I don't have bad luck! I could have sworn that you'd be with me, Jimmy! Let it go. You won't—no, I know that you won't talk about this, Jimmy."

He went off hurrying, as if for an appointment at which he already was overdue, while Jimmy Green looked after him.

The man for whom he had felt such shame, the trickster and cheap coward and juggler, Alabama Joe, was in the expectation of Charlie Dyce a criminal so great that his capture would mean fame and almost fortune for a young policeman.

The savor of this information made the very heart of Jimmy leap.

If Alabama was a criminal, it was too bad. But the shadowy world of crime did not appear in the eyes of Jimmy as it did to mature minds. It was, rather, a region of mysterious adventure, gun fights, daring marches, long rides on horses, heart-breaking expeditions beside a dog team. So Jimmy Green looked upon crime as a thing to be avoided, but also as a thing which might be admired, in a sense.

He came to a picket fence and went down it slowly, letting his finger tap on every picket. Far off he heard the weirdest cry in the whole wilderness—the booming call of a moose, and had a sudden picture in silhouette of a monster buried to the slender knees in mud and water, with his yearning head stretched out, and the shadow of his great horns dim in the water beside him.

But in all the wilderness there was nothing half so exciting as this affair of Alabama Joe, the beggar, the gunman, the juggler, the coward, the product of the underworld of crime —if such he were.

Jimmy could not, honestly, become a spy in the service of

Charlie Dyce, but his boy's conscience permitted him to d
just a little spying on his own account.

From Madame Duval, that night at supper, he had learned
that the big stranger not only had a job in the grocery store
but also that Bill Carson had given him the spare room in hi
own house, thereby being able to cut down the wages h
paid. Those wages, the widow understood, were almos
nothing.

"Trust a man with a red nose to drive a good bargain!"
she had said.

Jimmy Green, therefore, journeyed to the rear of the Car
son house.

He knew his way perfectly. There was hardly a backyard
in all of Fort Anxious with which he was not familiar. H
knew the wood piles, the sheds, the outhouses; the corrals
the berry and vegetable patches; the board fences which give
privacy, and splinters in the shins; the yards where savage
bulls may lunge at you; and the pens where a cross, hungry
old sow may bite off a foot as soon as you could say Jack
Robinson.

He managed to find his way over the first two fences. He
mounted the next fence and, just beyond, blundered against a
newly formed pile of boxes. One of these was dislodged, and
fell with a great rattling.

A window went up in the house with a bang—the window
of the lighted room.

"If you don't keep out of there, I'll fill your young hide
full of pepper and rock salt, Jimmy Green!" shouted the
grocer.

Jimmy shrank to the ground and rested there upon one
knee.

He thought for a moment that old Carson was possessed
by an evil spirit, to be enabled to see so far into the dark of
the night.

But then he understood. Carson had simply shouted out the
name which always was hitched to every stroke of mischief
in Fort Anxious—Jimmy Green.

Inside the house, the sweet, low voice of Paula Carson was
laughing, and Jimmy went forward again, reassured.

56

CHAPTER FOURTEEN

AFTER THAT MISADVENTURE with the box pile, you can be sure that the boy went as soft as a wing of night.

He looked into the dining room, where Bill Carson still remained in his shirt sleeves, biting his lips and chewing a pipestem over a newspaper which he pushed away from him from time to time and shook his head over. Jimmy could hear him saying: "Tut, tut!" and "Well, dang it all, would you think—"

Mature human nature always amused Jimmy—there was so much folly, so much apparent bad temper and real good nature. He regarded the fiery-faced old grocer for some time. It seemed to him that the red skin of the merchant must be giving out heat like the opened front of a stove. By his own excess of fire, Bill Carson must be frying in that room!

So thought Jimmy, and lowered himself cheerfully to the ground.

No big Alabama Joe was there!

Upstairs, however, a light shone. The thin shade was drawn down and a vague outline of a man seated at a table appeared there, as though Alabama Joe did not join the family in the evening, but retired to his chamber after meals, after the fashion of the usual hired man.

This made the boy shake his head. No matter how disreputable Alabama might be, the fact remained that he was fully the equal of the Carsons, so far as brains went.

Jimmy went up to look in at the window of the room upstairs. A squirrel could not have climbed with greater skill, with a softer touch. He went up a drain pipe from the gutter of the roof. He swung out to the sill of the window, and hanging there precariously, but unthinking of danger, he looked behind the shade, through the aperture, at the side.

There was no one in the room. The lamp burned with a slight flicker of the flame, and in the chair appeared an overturned box surmounted by a pillow with a string cinched into the top of it. The pull of the string threw up a roundness of about the size of a head, and this in turn cast the necessary shadow upon the shade.

In this manner was the room of Alabama Joe occupied, but of the man himself there was not a sign!

When Jimmy had seen this, he grew so frightened that he cast a sudden glance down at the ground. And the distance made his arms shake and almost give way beneath him. He barely managed to get to the pipe, and lowered himself slowly.

He had thoughts for every handhold that he took on the way down. Charlie Dyce had an eye in his head—that much was certain. And upon this proof of deceit alone, Jimmy was willing to spring to the conclusion that Charles Dyce was right *in toto*. A criminal, a dangerous man, masking behind the miserable part of an habitual coward.

He almost wished that he had not climbed up to peek into that room. And then he almost wished that he had accepted the offer of Charlie to play the spy. Neither wish did he keep more than a second.

Voices, in the meantime, were sounding from the front room, and Paula Carson was laughing, there.

The morals of Jimmy, which forbade him to spy in the pay of another, did not at all keep him from advancing to the front of the house and crouching on the porch outside the window of the sitting room.

He could see everything, for the curtain was not even drawn. He could hear everything, for the wall was a flimsy affair. What the boy saw inside made him open his eyes very wide indeed. For big Stanley Parker was in there alone with the girl, and it looked as though he was not making an idle call.

"Of course you don't," he was saying. He stood before Paula, while she sat with her head tilted back, looking squarely up at him. "You can't expect to so soon. All that I say is, keep me in mind. I'm no sentimentalist, Paula. You know that."

"I know that," said she.

"So when I say that I care a lot about you, I hope it means a little?"

"Of course it does," said she. "And when I think of what you mean in Fort Anxious, Stanley—"

"Oh, well," said he, generously waving aside that idea. "But the fact is, Paula, that I do mean a little bit. I'm going to mean more, and I want you to have whatever I can give you. I don't have to mince matters with you, Paula. Old

58

Tyndal has promised me everything. Matter of fact, he was impressed by that little ruction between me and Dillman, the thief."

"Every one was," said Paula. "No man in Fort Anxious ever did a braver thing!"

"That's nothing," said Stanley Parker. "The important thing is that Tyndal wants me to run the business. He's behind me. He said so only yesterday."

"Does he know that you think of me, Stanley?"

"He knows, of course. He's glad of it. He said that a humble wife would—I mean to say, Paula, that he agrees with me."

"Yes?" said she.

She looked at Parker and then over him, thoughtfully.

"He's talkin' down to her," said the boy to himself. "He's a fool, if he only knew it!"

Stanley Parker very apparently did not know it. For he went on, after a moment:

"Now, Paula, we ought to reach some sort of an agreement, it seems to me."

"What sort of an agreement, Stanley?"

"Why, about things in general. That you're to—well, let's say that you're to be seen with me a good deal—so that we can get people used to the idea of what's to come, and so that you and I can get better acquainted."

"I suppose that that's the most important reason," said the girl.

"As far as the debt of your father is concerned," said he, "I'll take care of that. Mr. Tyndal will do exactly as I say. We can eventually wipe that debt right off the books, Paula!"

He said it with a shining face and a click of the teeth. But she merely half-closed her eyes and a single line of pain appeared between her brows.

"Yes?" said she.

"But in the first place, Paula, I think it better that I should have something to say about the running of the business. There's no use letting it go on downhill."

"No," said she.

It was odd how she confined her conversation to monosyllables, thought Jimmy.

"I could give your father a good deal of advice. And a little advance of money to brighten up his store and his business. If he'll allow me to dictate how it should be spent. You understand, Paula. Of course, we can't have hobos like that fellow Alabama Joe— Is that his name?"

"Yes, that's his name," said she.

"We can't have creatures like that around. Plain tramp."

"Not a plain tramp," said she.

"What do you mean, Paula?"

"I mean that he's a very interesting fellow."

Stanley Parker made a wry face. "My dear child—" said he. Then, abruptly, he changed his tone. "I'm afraid that I shall have to be firm," said he. "I really am, Paula!"

"Yes?" said she.

"I'll have to put my foot down about that hobo! That cheap, worthless loafer!"

"He kept a crowd in the store all evening, and they bought no end of things," said Paula.

"The rascal juggled and took up a collection in the street."

"Did he?" said she. She seemed startled. There was a flush in her face.

"He did."

"A collection!" said she.

She was erect in her chair, now, not looking at Parker, but at the window outside of which Jimmy kneeled. There was an odd suggestion of dismay in her eyes.

"You'll have to take that up with Dad," said she. "You'll be wanting to get home to bed, Stanley. I don't know what to say to you—"

"You're tired," he broke in hastily. "Don't say a word. Don't be hasty. Ten million good opportunities have been thrown away by hasty answers, Paula!"

He looked a splendid fellow, standing there with his broad shoulders, and his handsome face, heavy about the jaws. He looked like a man who never could fail.

"I'll be as careful as I can be," said Paula. "I'll think it over all night, Stanley—"

A hand gripped the collar of Jimmy. He was lifted as if at the end of a derrick arm.

Twisting about, his knife unsheathed as readily as the claws of a cat, he saw the outline of big Alabama Joe, and the knife-hand of Jimmy was nerveless even before it was gripped in a powerful vise.

CHAPTER FIFTEEN

WHEN JIMMY WAS CARRIED off from that porch, he knew how a rabbit feels when a great horned owl strikes its talons onto the soft body and quickly swoops away with it.

He was so helpless that he stopped struggling in an instant. He never had felt such a grip, not even the hand of Awaskees, as it lifted him out of the rapids that unforgettable day when the canoe overturned. He stopped struggling, and he looked helplessly up.

It was a perfect night. The stars freckled all the sky, steadily shining. Far away, some French-Canadians were singing upon the river an old paddle song, giving it just the proper swing to make paddles drive in an effortless rhythm through the water.

In the nerveless blank of his mind, Jimmy Green noted these things.

Then he was put down under a tree. He was set free. Not even the deadly knife which dripped down from his hand was removed. But he did not attempt to stir.

A cold, wet thing touched his leg. It was the nose of Mishe Mukwa, sniffing him. No, Jimmy did not even dream of fleeing, but stood as if made of stone.

He waited.

So did the tramp.

It seemed to Jimmy, after a few moments of this, and of facing the silence of the big man, that he was growing brittle, freezing, so that the least stroke, the touch of a word would snap his will power in two.

"Porches," said Alabama Joe, "I always figured out, are dangerous places."

He waited again.

With great effort, Jimmy cleared his throat.

"Yes," said Jimmy.

"Especially this porch."

"Yes," said Jimmy.

"How much of that talk did you hear?"

"Not much, Alabama."

"Tell me how much."

"From the time where he told her that they ought to make a plan, to where he promised to fix up the store if her father would take his advice, and spend the money right, and fire you."

"That's the part you heard?" asked Alabama.

"That's all. Except when he left, she was to spend the night thinking things over."

Anger swelled in Jimmy, and it grew to such a high wave that he was able to forget his present danger.

"That's enough," said the tramp. "I don't wish to know what they were talking about; but I'm mighty surprised that an honest boy like you—"

"Dang him!" said Jimmy. "He's no good—I don't like him —he ain't half fit to marry her!"

"What a way," said the soft voice of Alabama, "what a way to talk about the leading young man of Fort Anxious, Jimmy. I'm surprised to hear this from you, Jim!"

"He's—I dunno," said Jimmy lamely. "I just don't like him!"

"Was that why you followed him here tonight?" asked Alabama.

"I didn't follow him," said Jimmy.

"Oh, didn't you? What brought you, then?"

"My legs!" said Jimmy impudently.

Something struck him along the side of the head. Not the open hand of Alabama Joe, surely, but a flexible steel cable.

He reeled, but he did not fall.

"If you speak like that to me again, I'll wring your neck," said Alabama Joe. "You came spying!"

Jimmy was silent. He was trying to readjust his thoughts, but the spinning of the stars into dim white streaks of fire disturbed him greatly.

"You came to find me," said the tramp.

Still, Jimmy did not speak. He gripped the handle of the knife with all his might, working his fingers a little. If that hand of steel struck at him again, he would strive to duck and hit in for the heart.

Yet he knew that he could not succeed. The time before, he had not even seen the flash of the hand before he received the blow.

"You came to find me," said Alabama Joe. "You've climbed up to my room!"

"Yes," said Jimmy.

"You saw what?"

"A dummy in the chair."

"Who sent you?"

Jimmy swallowed. He was glad that he had had a chance to talk a little, for it warmed him strangely, and enabled his mind to work more freely.

He felt that he could do something, now, before that terrible hand fastened on his throat, or the long, white teeth of Mishe sank in his flesh.

"Who sent you?" repeated Alabama Joe.

"No one," said Jimmy.

"You lie!" said the tramp.

He put a thumb into the tender flesh under Jimmy's chin and jerked his head up so short that the very roots of Jimmy's tongue were bruised. But, worse than this, as his head jerked back he found that the face of Joe was close to his, and even the starlight was enough to enable him to see its expression.

It curdled his blood. Once before, out there in the open meadow, he had seen something in this man like eyes in the dark. Now his soul turned to a bird ready for flight.

"Who sent you?" said the tramp. "Dang you, I'll have your heart out if you don't tell me!"

The lips of Jimmy parted. But he found somewhere strength in his sick heart and shut his teeth hard.

"Dyce sent you!" said Alabama Joe.

Again Jimmy struggled. It would be easy to shift the blame, but the lesson of his whole life rallied to him then.

"That's a lie!" said he.

He saw the shadow of the hand raised. He was nerveless and helpless to strike with the knife. So he looked straight back at Alabama Joe and waited for the finish.

Now, so suddenly that he staggered, he was set free.

"I never saw a gamer one," he heard Alabama Joe saying.

It was a mere mutter, but Jimmy could almost hear the singing of the spheres, at that moment, so acute were his senses.

"Jim," said Alabama Joe, "you came prospecting on your own account, is that it?"

He would have answered, feeling suddenly that he was to be allowed to live, but somehow he could not find words.

"Jim," said the tramp, "I'm a bad one, but I never was as

bad as this, before. I hit you, sonny. Here's my face. Whang me back, will you?"

But Jimmy put up the knife he had drawn. He was still very dizzy, and the stars wobbled in the sky.

"Are you done with me, partner?" said the soft voice of Alabama Joe.

Now, that touch of tenderness undid Jimmy Green more than the danger and the terror in which he had stood. He tried to clench his teeth. He tried to shut back the flood of weakness that rushed up into his throat. But, after all, he was not a man, no matter what he thought.

The sobs came violently. He struggled against them, he reduced them to a small pulse of sound, but he was helpless.

He found himself snatched up.

The dark head of Mishe Mukwa leaped up beside him, with a flash of teeth, but a whisper from the tramp ordered him down. And so Jimmy was borne swiftly away. Thick trees closed around them. The sky was shut out.

"Now let it go," said Alabama Joe. "If you've got tears inside of you, Jimmy, get rid of 'em. Cry if you have to. You're not a thousand years old, partner."

Again Jimmy struggled, but the low, choked sobs kept coming.

"I'm a dog," said Alabama Joe. "I'm a cur, and a low cur. I wish that you'd hit me across the face with a whip. Jimmy, I'm sick about it. You came to find out about me. I don't blame you. You're a boy, and a boy ought to skirmish on his own account! Jimmy, I'm sick. You want to know about me. Now you ask, and I'll tell you the whole yarn! Jim, what is it that you want, old son?"

"I'm ashamed," said Jim. "I'm most terrible ashamed, and I've—"

He mastered himself, dragging in great breaths.

"You saw the dummy in my room. But you saw it on your own hook. Nobody paid you to spy on me?"

"No," said Jimmy.

"I'd trust you to the end of time," said Alabama. "You can know whatever you please about me. Ask me, Jimmy!"

"I don't want to ask you," said Jimmy, gathering himself more and more.

"Will you forgive me, son?"

"I will," said Jimmy. "You caught me spying—you had a right—"

64

"To cane you, yes. Maybe. But not to use my hand on you —Jim, I'm a dog! You're the gamest lad I ever found. Jim, will you give me your hand?"

"D'you mean it, really and truly, Alabama?"

"I mean it."

The hand of Jimmy went out. It was taken in a careful but a mighty grip, soft as the hand of a woman, but prodigiously strong.

"I want you to know what you came to find out. I wanta introduce myself, Jim. I'm the Stingaree!"

CHAPTER SIXTEEN

It was that same day that he had heard the name for the first time, but somehow it had gone deeply into his imagination.

"I don't wanta hear your name!" cried Jimmy, clapping his hands over his ears too late.

For all the implications rushed over his mind at once. In the first place, he was bound by a pledged confidence and by the trust of the other to reveal nothing that he learned at this talk. In the second place, he could see exactly what was the course of the action to be: The Stingaree had come all this distance to the north in order to avenge the death of Bob Dillman, his old associate. For that reason he had asked all the questions about the killing of his old companion. Stanley Parker would have to die!

Not long before, Jimmy had been feeling that there was not a life which he would more willingly spare than that of Stanley Parker, but he suddenly thought of that glorious killing of Bob Dillman.

What could he do?

He could not reveal to Charlie Dyce what he had learned about the tramp. That would simply mean jail—perhaps the hangman's rope for Stingaree. Could Stanley Parker defend himself? Nobody, the boy was convinced, could stand for a moment against this man of mystery.

"You don't want to hear my name," said the tramp. "You've got reason, Jimmy. It's a bad name, and a black name, but I'd trust you with anything I know!"

"You've come here to murder Stanley Parker!" said the boy.

"It's hard to call it murder. Justice is what I've come with!" said the tramp.

"Justice!" said the boy. "You're gunna kill him, Joe!"

"Does he deserve to live?" asked the Stingaree bitterly. "He murdered Bob Dillman!"

"That was a fair fight. He didn't even have a gun!"

"Meaning, according to that yarn, that he took the gun away from Bobbie and then slaughtered him with it?"

"Isn't that what happened?"

"Listen, sonny," said the tramp. "Will you listen to me?"

"Sure, Joe."

"Stingaree is my right nickname."

"It sort of scares me to use it, though!"

"I knew Bob Dillman all my life since I was a kid younger than you. I was the boss of our town until Bobbie came along. We fought every night after school for a month. I never could lick him until he hit his head on a rock by luck—something the way that Larkin did today. I never licked him after that—we never fought. But Bobbie Dillman was more dangerous in a fight than any snake. He was quick as a wasp, and the sort of poison he carried, killed on the spot. He was a killer," said the Stingaree, with an odd touch of pride in his voice.

"A killer!" echoed Jimmy Green, turning faint again.

"He had eighteen men on his list," said the Stingaree.

"And how many have you got, Stingaree?"

"Me? Nothing to speak of, sonny. Nothing to speak of. Sometimes I've had to get out of a trap—but bullets knee-high are nearly as good as bullets through the heart. The other fellow may be keen on shooting, but he generally shoots a little wild after his blood has started running. But that Dillman, he loved a fight for the sake of fighting.

"Three men walked in on Bobbie one day when he was playing poker. They wanted him, and they wanted him bad. They came in from behind. But they didn't get him. One of them he shot through the shoulder, another through the stomach—he didn't die, somehow—and the third man got down and begged, and Bobbie turned him loose.

"Now, Jimmy, do you see the point that I make?"

"That he was a terrible dangerous man, Joe?"

66

"That his gun never was taken from him. Not even when he was asleep."

"But Stanley Parker got it!"

"Then it was given to him!"

Jimmy gasped. "I don't understand it at all!" said he.

"Double-crossing is all I mean," said Stingaree slowly. "Suppose he was behind—needed a little cash for something—went partners with Dillman, and while the cracking of that safe went on, Parker stood guard armed with Dillman's gun. Now do you see? It suddenly occurs to him that he has a chance to make a great name for himself, hypnotize Tyndal into making him his son and heir, or at least to pose as a hero. So he speaks to Bobbie, and when Bobbie looks up, he shoots him fair between the eyes. A good, cool, determined man, that fellow Parker. Otherwise, he would have tried for the body, and he would have shot more than once. I grant that Parker is a rare one, and that he gets what he's after. But the way that he got Dillman's gun was by a gift! D'you wonder that I'm here to square things up, Jimmy?"

There might have been other explanations, but Jimmy, as he listened, could think of none. He could see the picture of the deed; he could see Bob Dillman looking up suddenly from his work, with the wealth of the safe spread out before him, glorying in it. He could hear the very *crack* of the gun.

He had no doubt but that big Alabama Joe was right. Yet he struggled against the inevitable. He said:

"Joe, you ought to leave it to the law. It's really not your business to kill Parker."

"The law!" said Stingaree.

He laughed a little.

"The law!" he repeated. "It only sees where it wants to see. It's an owl. It flies in the dark. It hits when you're not looking. It wiped me out. I was straight. You hear me, Jimmy? I was straight as a string. I walked the chalked line. Nobody had anything against me. The crooks got at me. I had the goods on them, enough to convince any jury. But they dodged me in the law. They tied my hands. Should I sit down and cry? No, I stepped out and got my own back with a gun!"

"But Dillman," said the boy, "Dillman was a crook. You admitted that, Stingaree."

The Stingaree answered with emotion:

"He was my partner, Jimmy. What do I care what he did

67

to other people? He was straight to me. Twice he cracked tool-proof steel jails like sardine cans to set me loose. He staked me when I was broke. He gave me his coat in the cold, and he gave me his share of water in the desert. His gun was my gun. His fights were my fights. He stole for me, begged for me, fought for me. And now he's waiting out the dark to see how I'll settle the account."

Jimmy Green argued no longer, for he saw that words were useless.

"Stingaree," said he, "it's a terrible thing—murder!"

"No, no, Jimmy," answered the other. "I've never taken a man behind. I won't start in with Parker. He'll have his equal break. Is there any pleasure in dropping him in cold blood? No, Jim, but in telling him what's coming, and letting him play his hand for the sake of the money, the big reputation, and the girl! He's got enough to make him fight. And he can shoot straight. No, no—not murder, Jimmy!"

But he purred as he spoke, like a great, contented cat—it could not be called laughter that Jimmy was hearing.

And Jimmy could not speak. In fact, there was no answer to make, except to say:

"Will you be able to make him fight you?"

"Oh, there are ways of stinging any rat until it feels it's cornered and strikes back. I'll find the way to sting Stanley Parker!"

And Jimmy could not help believing that the other would live up to his word.

"What shall I do?" said Jimmy, groaning in his quandary. "Why did you tell me, Stingaree? Why did you put it on me? I'd rather you'd have wrung my neck, pretty near!"

"Because I wouldn't leave you out in the dark, Jimmy. Because you've been a partner to me here in Fort Anxious. That's why. You don't have to sneak around in the dark to find out what you want to know about me. Come and ask me straight out!"

They walked out from the trees.

"Good night, Jimmy," said Alabama Joe.

"So long, Stingaree," said the boy soberly.

They shook hands, and again the soft palm of the Stingaree seemed to the boy like the velvet touch of a cat's paw.

No further questions—no asking of pledges of silence—no taking of oaths—but all was left to the honor of Jimmy Green. That honor was bright as the moon!

Slowly he started back up the street, not even wondering where he should spend the night, when a form rose out of the brush, and a man with a long, light stride came up beside him.

Jimmy was not frightened. He had been through so much that day and night that a star could have exploded in the sky without making him so much as blink.

"Well, Jim," said the voice of Charlie Dyce beside him, "you're a regular owl. A late walker!"

"Yeah?" said Jimmy, uninterested.

"Jim," went on the other, "I've got this much to say to you. Partnerships are good things—if you get the right partner! That's all. So long!"

He went out through the dark, and Jimmy stared heavily after him. How much had Charlie Dyce heard, if anything? Something he certainly had seen!

But he went on, grimly shaking his head. His lips were sealed. Neither in Dyce nor in the Stingaree could he confide!

CHAPTER SEVENTEEN

ALL OF FORT ANXIOUS began going to the grocery store of Bill Carson. They came in droves. They came to see the big dog, Mishe Mukwa, lying in the window, with his forepaws crossed, and his eyes constantly following his master about the shop. It was said that Kite Larkin had accepted two hundred dollars for the dog from the tramp, and that Alabama Joe had raised the money by his evening exhibitions of juggling in the street. At any rate, Mishe accepted his new master with a great devotion. Everywhere, he followed the stranger, or lay at his feet and guarded them with a savage affection; only in the store could he be induced to lie on the shelf, merely snarling silently when he saw the crowd near Alabama.

The crowd came to see Mishe Mukwa, but still more it came to see Alabama Joe, now a full-fledged clerk in Carson's store. He had a word for every one. And every one came, every one lingered a little. It was like a perpetual sale, in the Carson store. Maker and Webb's store had no patrons, now! As for Bill Carson, he and his daughter were busy bringing and wrapping, but the new clerk did the selling and the delivering, and every night old Carson stood for a time, rapt, and stared at the heaps of coin that made his cash drawer heavy.

Jimmy Green came with others to the store, when he could snatch a moment from his other affairs. His dignity now towered higher than ever. For he had brought Alabama Joe to Fort Anxious and was known to be the closest friend of the big fellow.

So, on this morning, Jimmy sat on the window ledge beside Mishe Mukwa. The dog did not love him, but at least he had been induced to accept Jimmy's presence without anger.

Three trappers had come in, all of them looking for knives.

"The famous thinking knives of Bill Carson," said Alabama Joe. "You couldn't have come to a better shop." He took out a tray of them. "Always ready to your hand. Always anxious to serve. The famous thinking knives of Bill Carson! Take your pick, gents."

Three knives spun up into the air, and whirling down, lodged their points solidly in the face of the counter and stood there humming like three angry wasps. No other knives could even have been given to the trappers, after that. They took them out and thumbed the steel and swore it was a finer edge than they ever had seen before. They went away delighted.

Mrs. Jim Graham came in for laundry soap.

"It does the work for you," said Alabama Joe, bringing out some yellow cakes. "You turn out a laundry with this soap, ma'am, and it hurts the neighbors' eyes. Socks get bigger when you wash them with this soap. It's the kind of soap that the queens and the duchesses always use themselves for their handkerchiefs. 'Duchess,' says the queen, 'I never saw your handkerchiefs looking so white.'

" 'Use Young's Yellow Peril,' says the duchess.

" 'Thanks terribly,' says the queen.

"Nothing but Young's Yellow Peril inside royal palaces, Mrs. Graham. How's Jim?"

He kept talking constantly, not loudly, but rather in a friendly, confidential manner, and people doubled their purchases to hear more of his nonsense.

Old Ding Vincent came in.

"Have you got some honey?" said he.

"I have some honey," replied Alabama Joe. "Yes, sir, I have some honey what am. The only thing is— Do you keep bees, Ding?"

"Me? Why the heck should I keep bees?" asked Ding Vincent, wagging his beard as he shifted his quid.

"A good thing you don't," replied the salesman. "You take this honey we carry—when bees get a whiff of it they crowd around for a day or two and try to steal it, and failing that, they get downhearted. Their own honey don't taste so good to them, afterward. Seems moldy, and made out of glucose instead of meadow flowers, Ding. Those old bees begin to sit around and mope. They begin to feel that they never had the right start. First thing, they're dead. That's why I always hate to sell this honey to a beekeeper, Ding; but seeing that you don't keep them, here you are. You better take six bottles of it while they last."

"Young feller," said Ding, "don't this here bottle say 'imitation' right here on the label in small print? And ain't that why the dog-gone no-good stuff is so cheap?"

"Ding," said the clerk, "I'll tell you what it is. It's modesty, Ding. Anderson knows he's got the best honey in the world. But does he want to crowd out all his competitors? No. And that's why he puts 'imitation' on the labels."

"Gimme half a dozen bottles," said Ding. "You'd make cats vote for dogs for the town council, young man."

Down the river, the whistle of the lumber mill hooted like a great hunting owl; it was twelve o'clock, and the crowd in the store rapidly melted away. Only the two Carsons, Alabama, and Jimmy Green remained.

Bill Carson sat down with a grunt of weariness on an apple box.

"I gotta get in a new stock," said he. "I'm getting cleaned out. The boat oughta be up the river to the landing by next Wednesday, but I dunno that we can hold out that long. It's like a run on a bank; and there ain't any need of makin' everybody buy six of ever'thing, Alabama! It's a fool way, when the stock is nigh washed out of the cellar, and the attic, too!"

Paula Carson slumped into a chair, utterly tired out, and big Alabama Joe sat on the counter beside her, swinging his heels.

"Maker and Webb are dying of starvation," said he. "Jud Maker has taken in his belt five notches, and Jessica Webb is ready to take in washing. Hang on a little while, Carson, and they'll move out of town, and then you can raise your prices all around and get as rich as Croesus!"

Bill Carson listened with popping eyes.

"When I listen to you, young feller," he said, "I never can tell when you're advisin' me and when you're laughin' at me. The bees quit when they smell Anderson's Amber! Sure they quit! That stuff to be called honey!"

"Mind rules matter, you know," said the tramp.

"Where'd you hear that?"

"I read it on a poster. Paula, if I go to the dance tonight, d'you dare to dance once with me? Or will Stanley Parker let you?"

She looked in alarm toward the door and sighed with relief when she saw it was empty.

"Are you ashamed?" she asked him, flushing a little.

"I'm not," he answered. "I have a new suit. I bought it at the store yesterday. It's a little quick around the shoulders, and it'll show my cuffs, but that's fashionable. I've got an iron collar, too, and I've written the words on it."

"What words?" she asked him, smiling a little.

" 'His name is Alabama Joe. If found straying, please return to Paula Carson, Fort Anxious. Not valuable, but we love him.' That's what I've written, Paula."

"Hum!" said Bill Carson. "What kinda rot you talkin' now? The pair of you!"

"Are you going to the dance?" asked Paula.

"I am," said Alabama.

"Stanley Parker has my card," said she. "I think he's had the dances all filled on it."

"Which one with me?" asked Alabama Joe.

"I don't know," said the girl. "I hope that there'll be a place—"

"There will," said he. "You can make your choice. Waltz, two-step, or schottische. I've had a medal for two-stepping, Paula, and when I waltz you don't need music. But the schottische is my main hold, Paula. Slow and dreamy is my style, and every girl thinks she's Cinderella. You'd better ask for a schottische. I've still got a few left."

"What girl are you taking?" said she.

"I haven't read over the waiting list," said he. "But I favor Marie Dugommier. She's always smiled at me since I pulled the knife out of her mother's ear."

"Poor, dear Marie never has any clothes."

"Kindness is what I want," said he, "and small feet."

"You can't talk French," said she.

"That will leave more time for dancing. Shall I take Marie?"

"You're the judge," Paula answered, and Jimmy saw her head go up a little. "I don't have to dance with her."

"But we'll be sitting next to you and Parker," he replied.

She started. "How do you know that?"

"I'll put a bet on it, Paula."

She started up suddenly.

"It's time for lunch!" she said sharply. "Jimmy, are you coming with us?"

He followed, trailing far behind, very thoughtful.

He could guess that there would be excitement at that dance. Tragedy, perhaps? For the Stingaree would not wait much longer. Charlie Dyce was absent from the town and certainly Alabama Joe knew that the policeman had not left on a pleasure trip. At any rate, Jimmy decided that he would be present at that dance, no matter how hard it might be to climb to a window.

CHAPTER EIGHTEEN

WHATEVER FAULTS Stingaree found with his dress that night, Jimmy Green could think of none. For Alabama Joe had on a good suit of blue serge and if it were not exactly ample, it showed off all the better the ponderous width of his shoulders and the crease down the center of his back. This to Jimmy seemed perfection in a coat. He was in the room of the Stingaree, watching him get ready for the dance, and admiring, finally, the white flower which the man put in his buttonhole.

"You look mighty slick, Joe," he declared.

"Do I?" said the Stingaree. "This is a mighty bother, though!"

He took from the bureau drawer a revolver, and the eyes of Jimmy grew round as he looked at it. It had a long barrel, an obviously custom-made stock, and it possessed neither sight, trigger nor trigger guard. It was a single-action veteran, prepared for fanning and fanning alone. This weighty gun the Stingaree thoughtfully dangled and spun upon his finger tips. He opened the flaps of his coat, he shrugged his shoulders, and at last, taking off the coat again, he strapped around his left shoulder a small spring clip which hung under the left armpit. Into this he fitted the weapon.

"D'you have to have it?" asked Jimmy faintly.

"I'd feel undressed without it," said the Stingaree. "I wouldn't be at home in my own house!"

But Jimmy could not help guessing that the great moment was almost here when the Stingaree was to be seen in action. Somehow, he dared not ask a more pointed question. He saw Stingaree leave the room. He followed him and the big dog down the stairs, and watched the tying of Mishe Mukwa to the end of a strong chain. Then Alabama Joe went to find Marie Dugommier, and Jimmy Green started for the dance hall.

He had planned the maneuvers he would execute with the greatest care. The dance hall was simply the second floor of what had once been a big barn. On the ground floor there were two stores. The rent of these kept the whole place going. And so the upper floor was free for entertainments of all kinds.

Jimmy, to approach the barn, went around behind it. There was a huge pine tree growing there, bending over at a slant so distinct that its top leaned over the roof. Up to that top Jimmy went, and getting out on the perilous tip of a branch, it lowered him softly to the roof. He watched the branch jump up with a swish high above his head. It was easy to get here, but retreat would not be so simple.

His next advance was more precarious. He had to lie out on the rotten gutter of the eaves. The tin work and the wood groaned and ripped under his weight, but he was able to look over and find what he wanted. This was a fragment of an old ladder which went up the side of the barn.

By his toes he hung from the creaking, sagging eaves, and the trees and the street swung beneath him until he got a handhold on the ladder and came down on its length with a great jerk. He thought nothing now of passing from the ladder down to the level of the second-story windows and there crawling hand over hand along a meager ridge on the side of the building.

He gained in this manner the front of the corner window.

It was shuttered some three feet above the floor, and outside of the shutter was a shallow iron framework which left just enough room for Jimmy to accommodate himself between. He did not need to rise up and look over the shutters. He could simply sit there in a good deal of comfort and through the crevices of the shutters he was able to see and hear all the hall except for a couple of the most distant corners.

There was enough to fill his eye, however.

He thought that he never had seen anything so wonderful as the transformation in both men and·women. Taken singly, in the street, as he had seen them before many a time, the woodsmen and the trappers looked clumsy, their clothes too small, their faces exceedingly tanned, and their hands burly and unshapen. But in the mass, it was different. The light of three big clusters of oil lamps illumined the crowd. It made the young men seem like Apollos to Jimmy. And as for the girls, they fairly dazzled him. The very rustling of their dresses was enough to make a heart leap. And they wore special smiles which never came off.

While Jimmy was looking, with his heart knocking at his very teeth, old Mrs. Chris Muller and her daughter Helena took their stand just before the window, so that Jimmy grew dizzy and his neck ached from ducking to one side and then to the other in an effort to look past them.

"I never seen anything like the way that things are coming to!" said Mrs. Chris Muller.

"It's pretty terrible, all right," said Helena.

She shook her chin as she answered, and her second chin redoubled the negative. Of the real chin, there was not much; for Helena's face slid by easy stages and imperceptibly into her round, fat, shining neck. Her face did not begin to form an angle until it reached the line of her upper teeth, which projected in a massive, dazzling row. Helena always looked cheerful, because she could not help smiling.

"There's Flo Lawrence," said Helena. "She got a lovely smile, Ma."

"There ain't but one real smile in this room," said Mrs. Muller, with a resolute movement of her shoulders, "and there ain't but one set of teeth, neither."

Helena and her mother passed on, only pausing to embrace Flo Lawrence. Flo was pretty and petite. She had great big blue eyes, and she had a way of lifting them up the front of a man's coat, button by button, until at last she dawned on him

75

like a sunrise sky. She was dawning, just now, on young Chester, and he was staggered with the beginning of each day!

"Look at that poor Helena Muller!" said sweet little Flo. "She's got a mouthful, ain't she?"

"Yeah," said Chester, "she's gotta half dozen eggs in her mouth, I guess."

Chester drifted away. Angular Lilian Bayne came to the side of Flo.

"Lookit!" said Flo. "There's Marie Dugommier lookin' like a house on fire and—lookit! She's got—the *tramp!*"

CHAPTER NINETEEN

JIMMY CRANED his neck until it grew brittle. A tap would have broken it off short, like a stick of taffy candy.

Marie Dugommier came in laughing. Girls always came in laughing, for that matter. He could see them in the door take a breath and grit their teeth, so to speak, and then start their laughter as though they were coming onto a stage. But Marie Dugommier laughed in a different manner. She laughed, Jimmy felt, from her very toes. She had a hand shamelessly tucked inside the big forearm of the Stingaree. She was looking not around her, but up at him. As though she actually thought her escort might be a little better than a worm!

"Lookit her! Crazy about him," said Flo.

"It ain't none of my business," said Lilian Bayne. "Only I don't admire his taste none too much."

"Nor neither do I. Ain't he big though!"

"Yeah. He's big, all right. They say he's a common tramp."

"Yeah. Think of comin' to a dance with a tramp! You been to the store?"

"Yeah. Bill Carson has pretty near got rich, they say. The old cheat! Lookit! He's got a white flower in his buttonhole."

"He's wearin' a flower, like a girl. Think of that! I wonder Marie don't make him take it out!"

"She's so dizzy about her tramp that she don't see nothin'. Say, there's Paula Carson and Stanley Parker!"

"D'ye think it's true that they're engaged?"

"Yeah."

"I hope it ain't. He could do better than a grocer's daughter, I guess."

"Well, you take when a girl makes a dead set at a fellow, he ain't got much chance to get away!"

They drifted away, and the boy outside the window bit his lip with venomous anger. He would remember the pair of them—the wild cats!

But now, dazzling to his eyes, the main actors of the drama—so far as Jimmy was concerned—came to his very window, and sat in the chair beside it. Stanley Parker, tall and stately, aware of other people in the room only by side glances, and Paula Carson with him; and then the tramp, and Marie Dugommier. In four chairs, side by side they sat. Mr. Parker had taken his place first, with Paula, when the others came up, and he turned pink. Jimmy could guess that he would gladly have changed to more distinguished neighbors.

But the two girls began to talk in a rapid chatter, nodding and laughing together. They seemed great friends. Dimly, Jimmy remembered certain speeches of detraction which Paula had made about the other that very day. He sighed.

Mr. Stanley Parker and his partner sat out the first dance, and in spite of the music, and the bustling of dresses, and the scrape and whispering of many feet raking the floor, Jimmy could hear Parker laying down the law. He did it with a smile, but the smile was as cold as ice. It was disgraceful that a common tramp should be allowed to sit with the respectable members of a community. He hoped that she would speak to her father about this affair. That should be his cue to discharge the reprobate instantly!

And Paula? She listened with a downward head, speaking so softly a word now and then, that even the keen ear of Jimmy could not make it out.

They went off in the next dance together. Jimmy almost forgot the trouble in the air as he watched the strange process of this dancing, seeing men and women swirl in a great pool of which the music made the waves.

The hall was growing crowded, now. Jimmy saw nearly all of the young men and girls of the town. There were even some who rarely appeared, and among these were the Lafitte brothers. They must have learned that Mounted Policeman Charlie Dyce had gone out from Fort Anxious again, or surely they never would have dared to show their faces.

They had records, the Lafitte brothers. They had compiled

77

part of their records with guns, and part with knives. They were equally at home with both. They were pleasant-looking fellows, sleek, smooth, ready to smile. They could afford to be good-natured, people said, because they never worked! Here they were, floating through the crowd, picking up a dance here and there. But Jimmy noticed that when one of them danced the other remained in an obscure corner, from which he looked out warily, like a bird of prey.

The breath of Jimmy came fast and short. Sometimes he looked at the swirl of the dancers in general, and sometimes he picked out the forms of the Stingaree and of big Stanley Parker.

What would happen?

It came in a tag dance, the beginning.

It was all so casual that the boy hardly noticed, at first. He never had watched such a dance before, and he hardly understood, for a little, why it was that men gave up their partners when another man stepped out from the wall and tapped them on the shoulder. But he saw that through all the confusion of changes, Paula and Stanley Parker sailed around the room undisturbed.

And then Jimmy saw the big shoulders of the Stingaree coming through the crowd. Others might hesitate to bother Stanley Parker, but from the first moment, Jimmy had not the slightest doubt as to what would happen. The Stingaree was bent on taking Paula for at least a part of that dance.

So through the crowd he came, stepping lightly, gracefully, and reaching the pair as they spun by, he touched the shoulder of Parker.

Others saw it, too. Jimmy could spot the little look of wonder on the faces of many of the dancers, and instinctively they fanned back from Paula and her partner.

But they could be still more amazed to see that Stanley Parker did not give up Paula and step back from her. Instead, he went straight onward in the dance.

As for the Stingaree, he remained where he had been after first tagging Tyndal's heir. He stood there without apparent embarrassment, smiling about him, nodding here and there as acquaintances passed him; while Parker and Paula came by the near side of the room and Jimmy could see the frozen smile of the big man, and his concealed anger. He could almost read the mind of Stanley Parker.

A tramp had tagged his partner!

The whole room buzzed with it in a subdued fashion. And on they had to go, carried by the course of the dance like twigs on a whirlpool. They went by Alabama Joe again, and again he stepped a little forward and distinctly was seen to tap firmly on the shoulder of Parker.

But again the girl was not given to him!

Half the dancers sat down at once. Such an affair as this was a shooting matter; it was also a scene to be watched in security and quiet. But Stanley Parker, for a third time, circled the room with Paula Carson, and again he approached the spot where the big tramp stood at his ease, with the course of the dancers flowing about him on either hand.

For the third time he reached forth his hand, and this time Stanley Parker paused.

He had been holding in so long that he simply could not contain himself for another single moment.

His very voice escaped too loudly, and every person on that floor could hear him say:

"You danged loafer, get off the floor!"

CHAPTER TWENTY

FREE SPEECH IS the right of every man, and Fort Anxious was freer in this particular than almost any other place, but this was a little too much.

Jimmy felt a distinct freezing sensation, which passed upward from his spinal marrow to his brain.

However, there was no gun play.

The Stingaree simply was seen to bow, and as the dance ended at this moment, he came straight back toward the window, where pretty Marie Dugommier had been returned to her chair.

He stopped in front of her.

"Marie," said he, "I've been ordered off the floor. I wonder if you think that I should take you home now?"

Jimmy Green bit his lip in vast excitement. What would she say?

But she saw no more than others had seen. That the tramp was a coward, as he had demonstrated before in Fort Anxious. Her face was pale, but very set.

"You can do as you please," said she. "I'm not interested in that. I'm interested in the dance!"

It was even worse, in a way, than what Stingaree had taken from Parker. He took it, moreover, in exactly the same way. That is to say, he bowed to her, and this time he said: "Good night!" in the clearest and the most pleasant way, and then remained for a moment to say that he was sorry that he was forced to leave her, but he felt that authority ought to be obeyed by strangers in a new town.

Marie Dugommier kept her head high. She answered not a word, but looked straight through her escort, and Stingaree walked slowly from the room.

As he went, what a buzz went up!

There was only one important thing in the eyes of Jimmy Green, however, and that was the consummate ease of Alabama Joe. He was so far from being embarrassed that he could turn his head from side to side and, in his smiling way, mark down every face as he crossed the floor.

Alabama passed big Stanley Parker, too, coming toward the same corner which he had just left. Parker looked red and angry, and was very stiff in his walk. He had the air of a man who has done a very virtuous thing and doesn't care what the world thinks of it.

Passing him, the tramp was seen to pause for an instant, and say something, which Parker answered harshly, jerking his head over his shoulder.

Then Paula and her partner came on to the corner. She was white as could be. Jimmy heard her say:

"Stanley, I don't want you to go!"

"Be bearded by a scoundrel of a tramp? He wants the credit of having asked me out of the hall to meet him! I'll meet him! I'll—"

He swallowed the last words of his threat.

Paula Carson, regardless of the crowd, took him by both arms and held him an instant.

"Stanley," said she, "I don't want you to go!"

How wonderfully his face softened as he looked down to her!

"Are you really caring, Paula?" he asked her.

"He's dangerous!" said she.

"Paula," he insisted. "Do you care?"

"I'd care about any man!" said she.

He shrugged his shoulders and stiffened like a ramrod.

"I've got to see what he wants!" said he, and turned on his heel.

Jimmy turned, also.

He had to get down from that precarious eagles' nest of his with nothing but thin air under him, most of the time, but he managed it and in his excitement hardly realized that he had done a dangerous thing.

He got to the ground, hesitated a part of a second to draw his breath, and then bolted for the front of the barn.

There was a crowd there beside him, and that crowd was constantly added to by the numbers of people who boiled out from the door of the dance hall.

The light came from a pair of big oil lanterns over the doorway, the illumination tangling through the branches of the trees and casting a great spotted pattern on the face of the house across the street. That house was vacant, the shutters closed. It looked to Jimmy like the face of death.

And death, he knew, was in the air.

He gave that thought and that picture one glance, turning back to the barn itself, and the group outside it—the men, the excited, pleased faces of men waiting to see a fight, and the horses at the hitching racks tossing their heads so that their eyes flashed like metal in the light.

A comfortable and homely sight, that.

And upstairs, the methodical orchestra was beginning the next dance, a schottische!

He remembered what the tramp had promised Paula Carson—that he would dance a schottische with her, that night!

There was Alabama Joe himself, building a cigarette with deft hands, looking bigger, sleeker, than ever, and always with a good-natured smile.

"You'd better get out of here," some one told him. "That Parker is bad business to tangle with!"

"I'll get out as soon as I've finished this smoke," said he. "Always hate to smoke when I'm walking; it gets too much into your lungs, that way." He smiled as he said it.

They began to fall back from him and make a little circle.

And into that circle marched Parker with great strides.

He marched up to the tramp and confronted him, letting a pause of a second or so endure while he overbore the other with his mere presence. He stood close. Big as the Stingaree was, this other towered over him a pair of vital inches. He outbulked the tramp, too, with his high head, and his fine, square shoulders.

But Stingaree did not wince back, nor did his expression change; but his calm eye and his smile still traveled up and down the form of Tyndal's heir.

"You wanted to see me?" asked Parker loudly.

"I wanted to see you," said the tramp genially.

"Because I ordered you off the floor, I suppose? I'll tell you this. We don't explain our reasons when we give orders to our dogs, in this part of the world; and some people are no better than dogs!"

Words were forming and struggling in the throat of Jimmy, he wanted to shout out. He found himself murmuring distinctly: "You fool! You fool! You're half an inch from dying."

He spoke loud enough to disturb an iron-faced forester who nudged him fiercely and said: "Shut up, kid, and let the show go on!"

Jimmy hardly felt the shove or heard the words, so intently was he dwelling upon the faces and the words of the main combatants.

"Am I a dog, Parker?" asked the tramp mildly.

"You're little better," said Stanley Parker. "If I had my way, I'd whip you and your kind out of Fort Anxious and every other decent town in this country!"

"You'd whip me out?" asked the other, shaking his head and still smiling—in depreciation of the mildest sort.

"Yellow!" snorted the forester softly, in his deep disgust. "There ain't gunna be no fight at all!"

"Well," said Alabama Joe, "you talk like a judge, Parker. But I'd like to know your right."

"You'd like to know what?" roared Parker, coming within a foot of the tramp's face, his fists clenched.

But Alabama neither made preparations for defense nor shrank back. He merely said: "You gotta great big reputation up here, Parker."

"What has that got to do with you?" demanded Parker.

"That's what I want to know," said Alabama Joe. "It's a strange thing what makes a reputation in some parts of the world. Down in my neck of the woods it's one thing. But up here it's another. Up here all that a fellow needs to do, it seems, is to borrow a man's gun—and then murder him with it!"

Every word was clearly spoken, but an instant afterward, all that Jimmy could remember was that one word: "Murder!"

It rang out, somehow, in spite of the fact that it was not loudly spoken. It dwelt like an echo under the trees.

"Murder!"

It was big Parker who gave back, now.

He went back a whole stride, like a man who has been staggered by a heavy blow, and his face was the ugliest thing that Jimmy had ever seen, it was so white, so drawn.

"Murder?" said Parker in a gasp which undoubtedly he had meant to be a roar. "You cur, are you referring to Bob Dillman?"

The answer of the tramp was a marvel of its kind.

He flicked the ash from his cigarette, actually looking down to do so, and then he drew in a breath of smoke—and breathed it out straight into the face of Mr. Stanley Parker.

"Boy," said he, "Bob Dillman would have eaten three slow-footed curs like you and never have known that he'd dined. You never had the heart to stand to him. You're only brave enough, Parker, for murder!"

Once again that word hung in the air, like smoke from a gun.

This time it took Parker not altogether unprepared. His voice was something between a groan and a roar, and he smashed his fist straight at the tramp's head.

Now, Jimmy had fought many a battle in water and dry land, and he knew that the punch which lands is the one that starts no farther back than the hip.

He himself could have avoided this blow, this swinging, ponderous effort, without trouble. But the tramp did not dodge back. Instead he swayed his head to the side, and as the heavy fist shot past his ear, he stepped in—stepped up and in like a dancer rising on his toes; and as his weight descended to his heels, his hand—his left hand it was—jerked over the big shoulder of Stanley Parker and dropped on the side of his jaw with an impact as audible as the clapping of two open hands.

Stanley Parker crumpled to his face.

CHAPTER TWENTY-ONE

Would they know him now?

As he stepped back, it seemed to Jimmy that the murmur from the crowd must be saying softly: "The Stingaree!"

But they were saying nothing at all. They were simply gasping—and most of all, those stalwart lumberjacks who had seen the massive fists of Parker at work before this night. They had seen him crush the heroes of bunk houses and log drives. They knew him as an unbeaten man, and lo! at a stroke, the bubble was pricked, and he lay ruined in the deep velvet dust of the street.

If that was not enough to tell them, should they not have guessed, when they saw the tramp stand in his place, looking down to Tyndal's heir, and raise the undiscarded cigarette to his lips for another thoughtful puff?

He had not dropped it in the encounter. He had known that one blow would be enough. And he was right.

No common man could have dealt such a stroke. Certainly not one man in a million could have been so sure of the result! But still they did not guess. They did not know, on the whole, about the Stingaree, perhaps.

And yet it was wonderful that the tramp should have mentioned Bob Dillman before he fought. It was giving away his secret hand. It was placing his cards upon the table. It was letting the world see him, if the world cared to stop and think what was before its eyes.

The world, on the whole, apparently did not care to pause; but there was at least one Charlie Dyce who would understand in one instant, when he heard this reported.

So Jimmy drew his breath, and saw the future in the present moment.

No one moved, at first, until the tramp stepped back a little, and said:

"If there are any friends of this fellow around here, they might as well pick him up before he strangles in the dust."

Several went in, at that, and raised the fallen man.

He was quite unconscious. The blow had landed on his jaw, but the shock of it, or of his fall to the ground, had started his nose bleeding. Some one brought a can of water and threw it into his face.

Then every one scattered back.

They did not care to be seen by the heir of Mr. Tyndal as witnesses to the fall of big Stanley Parker. They fell back, and Parker got staggering to his feet.

He was still quite at sea. His breath came audibly, in faint groans. Then he came to himself with a start, when he nearly had run into the tramp. He recoiled and almost fell in his effort to get away from Alabama Joe.

"You?" said he, in drunken bewilderment.

The voice of Alabama sobered him at once.

Said the tramp: "Go home and get your gun, son. Bring it here and you'll find me easy to get at. Or I suppose you'd prefer to send a couple of murderers to finish me off?"

At this, with the red still trickling on his dusty face, Parker got himself together, stared a moment at the other, and then turned and went hastily off down the street.

Every one looked after him, bewildered, and Jimmy saw him tapping the pickets of a fence with his extended hand, like a boy going home from school. It made Jimmy sigh to think that even Stanley Parker had one day been as other boys, without a great disgrace hanging upon him. Now, he had been beaten once, and must fight for his life to redeem the disgrace.

Even with a gun, indeed, he could never recapture the lost ground. To do that, he should have leaped at the throat of the tramp like a tiger, the instant he recovered his senses.

Such was human glory, thought Jimmy, though in other words. That very evening, there had been in Fort Anxious no man so envied as young Mr. Parker. That moment, there was no man who would have stepped into his shoes!

And then the crowd swerved in around the spot. They talked, and Jimmy's poisoned ear could hear only one word over and over:

"Murder?"

Had Bob Dillman been murdered—and not killed in fair fight? The accusation had been made, and all the conduct of Parker seemed to support that accusation.

A hand touched the shoulder of Jimmy Green, and he turned to look up to the face of the tramp, not smiling, now.

"Jimmy," said he, "did you see it?"

"I saw!" said Jimmy hoarsely.

85

He followed the big man into the deepest shadows among the trees.

"He's going to murder me, now, if he can buy guns enough to do it," said the tramp.

"Get out of Fort Anxious, Joe!" said the boy, panting with his eagerness.

"I'm trapped," said the other, surprisingly. "Charlie Dyce is closing on my trail. If I leave, I get into deep woods, or rivers, or what not. I know the map, but not the land. I'm not a woodsman, and they'd run me down in no time. Jimmy, I've got to leave, but it will be hard sledding, unless I have a guide."

"I'll get you one!" said the boy.

"That Awaskees that I've heard you talk about?"

"Yes. I'll get him!"

"Then get him for me now. Offer him any money that you want for a reward—"

"He'll go because I tell him to go!" said the boy proudly. "But you come with me, Joe!"

"Ah, and I'd like to!" said the other. "But I don't dare, Jim. I've got to stay here."

"Why, why?" stammered the boy.

"Well, because I've given my word to Paula Carson that I'd dance a schottische, and I'm a crook who always keeps his promise, Jim!"

He laughed a little as he spoke.

Jimmy went nearer to him and gripped the big, soft, smooth arm. No one could have guessed at its strength.

"He does mean murder, Joe!" said he.

"I saw it in his face," replied the other, "but I've got to take my chance. Who is he likely to buy for the job? Can you tell me that?"

"I don't know!" said Jimmy. "There's some that would do it cheap."

"He won't trouble about the price, Jim."

"Get out of Fort Anxious!" begged the boy. "Get out! I'll have Awaskees for you! Joe, get out of the Fort."

"She'll expect me, Jimmy! She's wondering right now not so much how the fight is coming out as whether or not I'll come back to dance with her!"

"She knew how the fight would come out before ever it started," said Jimmy.

"D'you think so, son?"

86

"I heard her beg him not to go."

"In spite of those big, broad shoulders? Ah, Jim, there's a woman! Her like isn't born twice in the same century! But tell me one thing before you go for the Indian. Can you guess who he might hire? Can you give me a hint? I walk in the dark. Another week and I would know this town, but I couldn't wait another week. Not with Dyce on my back trail. I've left too many signs, in my life, Jimmy. Even a child could follow my spoor now! Tell me who to guess at?"

The mind of Jimmy whirled.

Before it passed in swift review the faces which he knew in Fort Anxious, the faces which he had known in the dance hall, smiling, gay, or grave. Then he cried out softly:

"Henri and Simon Lafitte!"

"Ah? Who are they, Jim?"

"They're small and sleek looking. Something like you, only smaller."

"Thanks!" chuckled the tramp, without malice.

"They've got black hair and eyes, though. Sort of ratty eyes, Joe. You'd know them if you saw them! Go upstairs and get somebody to point them out!"

"I'll know them well enough by this," said the tramp through his teeth. "And heaven keep any small, sleek-looking, black-haired man from making a hip movement tonight, so long as I can see him! Go on, Jim, and get Awaskees for me!"

Jimmy turned away, but he did not go at once.

Instead, he waited for a moment to see the crowd dissolving before the door of the barn.

In a way, this flurry which had meant the death of Stanley Parker's reputation had been no greater or more permanent than a whirl of dust and dead leaves, which eventually are scattered and leave no trace behind them.

So the crowd was now pouring back into the barn door, as though the whole affair had been nothing.

Nothing to them; but to Stanley Parker, more than life and death itself.

For Jimmy could picture him sitting in his room with his head in his hands, wondering how he dared to face the world the next day, wondering who would next accuse him of having borrowed from Bob Dillman the gun with which he killed him.

Or, instead of pondering, was he as the tramp suggested

87

now hiring murderers to wipe out the man who had shamed him?

Jimmy took a quick, deep breath. He glanced behind him once more, saw the lamplight of the doorway glinting on the smooth head of the Stingaree, and then bolted down the street to find Awaskees, the Cree.

CHAPTER TWENTY-TWO

THE LODGE of Awaskees was back toward the verge of the trees. He had a bit of land which he called his own and which nobody cared to challenge his right to at that moment. So that was his home.

It was the cleanest and best-kept lodge that Jimmy knew about. Awaskees, the great hunter, kept the meat pot filled with the best and in the utmost plenty. He was more looked up to than any other red man within five days' march. And that was true not only among the whites but among his own kind.

Awaskees was twenty-five years old, and since he was twenty, he had killed one man each year regularly. Not because he was quarrelsome, but because he often possessed things which the lawless envied.

Once it was his handsome young squaw, as tall as Awaskees, and with a grip of iron, as unlucky Jimmy very well knew. Once it was a pair of his best bear traps. At another time one of his winter caches had been opened and the food not replaced before the fall of the year. For every killing of which Awaskees was guilty, there was a very good excuse. Charlie Dyce was in the habit of saying that a couple hundred men like Awaskees would be enough to police all Canada, from San Juan de Fuca to the Thousand Islands, and the Mounted Police could be dispensed with.

Red men feared and loved Awaskees. White men feared and respected him. His word was as strong as a file of soldiers, and his gun shot as straight as a beam of light.

Jimmy he had taken as a sort of younger brother in the former's infancy, and ever since that moment, he had been unfailing and true to the white boy. He had opened his pack of most intimate hunting secrets. And he thought so much of his pupil that it was he who had said that "Jimmy Green can hunt moose!"

That is the highest compliment to be heard in the Northland.

So Jimmy went confidently along until his swift step took off the street, and down a twisting little lane, crooked as a cattle trail, and so to the inlet of meadow among the trees where he could see the fire glowing in the tepee.

When he came to the entrance, he knocked on a board which hung there. He knocked very softly, for he could hear a voice singing inside. Then he pushed aside the entrance flap.

Opposite him was a very old Indian, called altogether Flashing Hail in the Dark of the Night, though most even of the Indians shortened this to Flashing Hail.

His long hair, thick and glossy as the locks of a youth, tumbled down far beneath his shoulders, which were bare, and withered and shrunken with excessive age. It was Flashing Hail who sang, regardless of the two-year-old son of Awaskees, who hung onto the hair of the old man as though onto a rope and jerked and struggled with it with all his might.

The mother, now and then, mildly, attempted to free him from this annoyance; but she was afraid, obviously, of making the youngster start to shrieking. It was apparently better to let him tug at the hair of Flashing Hail than to interrupt the chanted story of the old man.

So only now and then she put out her strong hand tentatively. The rest of the time she was devoted to her beadwork, which she worked with the finest and brightest beads that she could get. This design was almost entirely red. Sometimes it seemed that her hands were filled with fresh, shining crimson fluid.

As for Awaskees himself, he sat in his usual manner, bolt erect, his arms folded, no pipe to fill his hands. His eyes were fixed before him. He saw the past.

Jimmy, entering, side-stepped hastily from in front of the withered arm which old Flashing Hail was stretching out toward the images of his story. Covertly the boy made the signs of greeting, and sitting on his heels, listened to the concluding phrases.

It had to do with a war excursion of his youth against the villainous Ojibways, thieves and murderers! On this occasion the valor and the cunning of the old man had taken a whole canoeful of furs and trophies from an Ojibway village, to say nothing of a very neat pair of scalps! To the words of the tale, the boy listened hardly at all, but kept his attention fixed upon the enchanted face of his friend, Awaskees.

The tale ended. Still, Jimmy dared not speak until Awaskees had withdrawn his eyes from the past and brought them down to his young guest with a frown and a sigh. Some great dream had vanished, and this was the awakening.

"Brother?" said he to Jimmy.

The latter hastily motioned the brave to follow him from the tepee. In the open, Awaskees took a few paces from the lodge, and then looked back toward it with another sigh.

"What is it?" he asked. "How has he come into trouble?"

"Who?" asked the boy.

"The big man—your new man, Jimmy."

"Why," asked Jimmy, "do you think that I've come for him?"

"If you had come for yourself, there would have been others at your heels."

Jimmy grinned in the darkness. To cover the eyes of this hunter was impossible.

"Also," said the Cree, "it is a bad thing for a man to go out of his range, to the south, or to the north. Your friend has come too far north!"

The truth of this, the youngster could not deny. He remembered the step of the tramp in the woods, and the crackling of the twigs beneath his feet.

"He's fought with Stanley Parker," said Jimmy. And he explained what had happened, together with his desires, which were that Awaskees should guide big Alabama Joe safely out of Fort Anxious and through the wilderness to the south.

"He will kill, my young brother," said Awaskees, when he had heard the whole story, "and because of the killing some one else will have to die. If I go with him, perhaps it will be I!"

Jimmy caught an impatient breath.

"You don't know that there'll be a killing," he said. "I don't think that there will be one! He flattened that Stanley Parker so hard that you can bet Stanley won't wait if he sees Alabama coming at him again. It was a terrible whang! Well, with Parker keeping out of the way, there should be no killing."

"Why didn't your friend use a gun instead of his fist? That would have finished the matter at once."

"He would have used a gun, if Parker had pulled one. But Parker didn't. And Alabama Joe is square, and wouldn't take advantage of a bobcat even. He gives every one a square break!"

"Ah," said Awaskees. "So does the rattlesnake. He gives a warning, because God put poison in his tooth. Does your friend carry poison also?

"Besides," went on Awaskees, "if he does not kill Stanley Parker, he may kill some other man. He is not one to come such a long march and then go back without a scalp. No, no, Jimmy. This is a man who never goes on the warpath without bringing home stolen horses, or scalps, or medicine bags——"

"What are you talking about, Awaskees? He's not an Indian!"

"Ah, no," said the Cree. "He's not an Indian. But he has counted many a coup on dead men and living men, brother. You can be sure of that!"

"What makes you think so, Awaskees?"

"Whoever looks at his eyes is sure to see the same thing. There is no doubt that one who has killed many times has a different eye. He looks through the window and he sees all the house inside."

"I don't know what you mean, Awaskees."

"Well, Jimmy. I shall make medicine, and see whether or not I go!"

He went back into the tepee. Jimmy followed only to the door, where the Cree paused, and scooping up a shallow handful of dust, he blew the dirt away and left the small pebbles only. These he counted, shifting them in his hand so that the firelight which streamed out around the edge of the tepee flap would strike on the bright little stones more clearly.

Then he tossed the pebbles high into the air and hurriedly dusted his palms together.

"Come," said he. "I shall go with you."

"It may be a long time, Awaskees. Are you going to speak to your wife?"

"She would howl," said the Indian, "and that is hard to bear. I have a canoe in the river. That is filled with my pack and everything that I need. Walk on, Jimmy. I only go into the lodge to get my rifle and ammunition and my wife will think that I am going to hunt moose under the stars."

CHAPTER TWENTY-THREE

THE ADHERENCE of Awaskees to his plan made Jimmy feel much lighter of heart, and he went on up the street with a cheerful swing to his shoulders, as though the battle were already almost ended. In this manner he left the alley, and stepping out into the street, he neared a group of half a dozen men. He stepped into a yellow arm of lamplight that streamed from a window across the street.

"Get that boy!" said the brisk voice of Charlie Dyce.

Two of those shadows sprang pantherlike. Jimmy was seized upon and dragged before Mounted Policeman Charlie Dyce.

In uniform now! And so were the five who stood around him. Six Mounted Police—more than would be sent out to put down a rebellion in a whole province. Jimmy had never seen such a sight. The presence of six Olympian gods could not have impressed him much more.

"Is this a joke, Charlie?" asked one of the men.

He wore a beard, and he had a deep voice. He was as big a man as Stanley Parker.

"That's the kid I told you about," said Charlie Dyce. "Keep that youngster under a blanket, and we've taken his eyes away from the tramp. Here, Jolly. Keep this boy for us. Treat him well, but keep a good tight grip on him. He's more slippery than an eel and a good deal cleverer than a ferret or a fox. Don't hurt him, though. Jimmy," he went on, "I'm sorry to do this, but I know that you'd try to help Alabama Joe. You'll hold this against me, till you're a good deal older, but I'll explain this much—I've found out about this new friend of yours!"

"What?" asked Jimmy defiantly.

"He's as bad as they make 'em, Jim. He's wanted all over the United States. He's wanted in Canada, too. If you put side by side all the safes that he has cracked, Jim, you could pave this street with 'em. He's robbed trains, stuck up stages, and filled up the dull times with a few gun fights here and there. South of the Rio Grande they want him badly. And all through the South they want him. You may even have heard of his best nickname clear up here. He's the Stingaree!"

He made a little pause, but Jimmy said not a word. He was not surprised. He was already contriving desperately how he might be able to break away from this captor and give the warning to Alabama Joe.

"Now then," said Charlie Dyce, "if you fellows will let me take charge for a while—"

"Go on, Charlie," said one of the men. "I hope that the next job won't be handling another youngster like this, though."

"We have time on our hands," said Dyce, "since we've got the boy safe. He was the ear and the eye of the Stingaree, believe me! We've got to get to Stanley Parker first. We'll post a couple of men at his house to guard him. Then the rest of us go down and pick up the Stingaree at the dance. I don't understand that dance business, though. Why should he want to waste time at a place like that?"

"Girls at the dance, Charlie. And the hardest of them are likely to soften a little about the women."

"I'm sorry, Jim, old son," said Dyce again. "Stand tight here. Jolly, take good care of him."

Charlie Dyce went off, and his companions with him, while big Jolly, he of the beard, drew Jimmy off the street and into the brush a short distance.

"Now, son," said he, "we'll stay here quiet, and no matter how much you want to help your partner, you've a pretty good excuse for standing quiet. No use butting your head against a wall, is there?"

"No," admitted Jim and sighed deeply. "I can't fight six Mounted Police, Jolly."

"No," chuckled the other, "you can't."

Jimmy Green began to whistle, letting his song trill higher and higher until it ended with half a dozen quite shrill and piercing notes.

A hard-palmed hand was instantly clapped over his mouth.

"Are you trying to send out a call for help?" demanded Jolly. "I'll have to gag you, youngster!"

"That was only an old paddle song," said Jimmy, lying as smoothly as an old practitioner. "And that end is the way the voyageurs yip. It don't mean nothing special."

"No more whistling," said Jolly sternly, "and don't talk louder than a whisper. You hear?"

"Sure," said Jimmy Green. "I'll do anything that you say!"

But, nevertheless, he was fairly trembling with eagerness to repeat that shrill phrase at the end of his song. It was the old rallying call of his crowd, which meant, to put all its meaning into words: "I am in terrible trouble. All good boys of the band help me. No little ones. This is man's work!"

There was all of this meaning in the signal, but, given only once, it was hardly likely that help could find him.

And, in the meantime, the strong hands of the law were closing in around Alabama Joe. Jimmy thought of the big, smooth, smiling face, and his heart was stirred.

"This Stingaree," said he. "Is he a bad one?"

"Him? I'll tell a man!" answered Jolly.

Jimmy turned cold with excitement. For down the street he saw three boys running as teal fly—in a rapidly changing, staggered flight. They were hunting for sign of one sort or another. Would Jolly notice them?

They halted at the corner and one of them dropped flat on his face. He was listening, of course. Ah, to be able to raise that whistle once again!

"What are those kids looking for?" asked Jolly suspiciously.

"Them? They're playin' Injun," said Jimmy Green. "They gotta fool game of Injun. I never seen nothin' in it, but a lot of 'em get out at night and run around like a pack of loons. It's sure a terrible surprise to me, Mr. Jolly, to find out that Alabama Joe is the Stingaree. Why, that's Bob Dillman's partner!"

"Yeah," drawled the policeman. "A mighty good partner, too. And he'll send that Parker fellow where Parker sent Dillman, unless we look alive. A good job that Charlie Dyce is tackling tonight, and I hope that he handles it. It'll make a name for him!"

"I bet it will," said Jimmy. "Well, I'm sorry for Alabama Joe. But I guess he's got it coming to him."

"Nobody more," said Policeman Jolly. "He's raised the deuce. But he's left a clean trail, I gotta say."

"Clean?" queried Jimmy, only half hearing—for yonder in the brush he heard the softest rustling like that made when a rising wind touches the bushes.

"Clean—no blood on his trail," said Jolly.

"I thought you said that he'd done his share of killing?"

"Crooks and thugs," said big Jolly. "They've backed him against the wall a couple of times and tried to pick his feathers, but he's been able to handle himself. I mean there's

94

no blood of honest men. Have you heard what he did in Taintorville?"

"No. Never heard of that town."

"It's down in Nebraska somewhere, I think. Three detectives cornered him. He stood their fire and wouldn't shoot back, except once high over their heads. Half the town joined in that chase, but he got away."

"How? How?" asked Jimmy eagerly, raising his voice a little to cover the noise of covert approach on at least two sides of them.

"That town backs onto a cliff, with the river underneath. Must be a fifty-foot drop, according to reports. And that fellow dived from the cliff, with bullets combing the air all around him."

"Fifty feet!" gasped Jimmy, remembering his own high dive.

"They thought he'd sure broke his neck. But when they looked down into the swirl of the river they couldn't see clearly. It was evening, d'you see?"

"Yes," said Jimmy. "Take him!"

He said it not loudly.

"Take what?" asked Jolly, without suspicion.

But out of the brush around them arose three forms of stalwart lads and dived at Mounted Policeman Jolly at the same instant. He was a big man, and a strong man, but a hundred-odd pounds smartly struck him behind the knees and made his legs sag at the same moment when a husky fourteen-year-old landed on his chest and beat him back. He went down before he could take his hand from Jimmy's neck and get out a gun.

He went down with such a thud that the wind was knocked out of him, and when he got back his breath, he was already tied hand and foot, for the nefarious followers of Jimmy Green carried tiestrings like so many cowpunchers at a round-up.

He was thoroughly tied and lay gasping on his side, while Jimmy Green in person kneeled beside him.

"Listen, Jolly!" said he.

"You dang little traitor!" groaned the big fellow.

"If we gag you, it might strangle you. Will you promise me not to call out for help?"

"I will."

"Then let him lie here. Jolly, I'm mighty sorry."

The four boys gathered on the edge of the street. There was hardly time for Jimmy to pant out his words of praise. Then he said:

"Here, Mike. You and Sammy get across the river. There's two mounted policemen at Stanley Parker's new house, guarding him. Find out where they're posted. Spot 'em, and then wait at the entrance. I dunno. Maybe we'd better find out about 'em. Pierre, you made a great tackle. Now hoof it for the dance. This late, they'll let you get up to look in at the dancers from the anteroom door. Spot big Alabama Joe and tell him that I'm waiting for him in the street. Life and death!"

CHAPTER TWENTY-FOUR

YOUNG PIERRE ran well. He got so far ahead—for Jimmy jogged on, full of dubious thoughts—that the chief of the band arrived in time to see his lieutenant thrown bodily out from the front door of the dance hall.

They were not allowing small boys to peek in on this night! Jimmy wasted no time.

Somewhere in the dark of the night Mounted Policeman Dyce was laying his plans and spreading his net. There was only one hope—that Dyce would trust to the capture of Jimmy and take too much time for his work. In that hope, Jimmy now rushed on to give his warning.

He only paused near the door to ask if big Alabama Joe were still inside, and was told that he was.

It was long-necked, grinning, peanut-headed Buff Logan who gave him the wanted information.

"Your friend's a great liar, Jimmy!" said he. "He's told Paula Carson that Stanley Parker had to go home and left him in charge of her; and there he's sitting between dances, talking to Paula on one side, and the Dugommier girl on the other, and everybody else in the hall knowing why Parker went home—but not Paula! Listen here, Jimmy—what was that that Alabama Joe accused Parker of doing to Dillman? Double-crossing, was it?"

"Aye—double-crossing."

"I never trusted him. He's got too much front, that Parker!" said Logan.

That, Jimmy hoped, would be the general feeling. In the meantime it was his duty to get into the dance hall, no matter at what risk. So he scampered back to the same tree which had been his ladder to scale the height before.

Up it he went. Gritting his teeth, blinding himself, he went steadily forward, and so gained the upper and outer branches.

The wind had risen. The bough on which he lay, grasping the outer twigs, tossed wildly and with the perversity of a bucking horse rather than with any regular and reasonable rhythm. He was so frightened that he could remember nothing in his life half as bad.

He turned and struggled back to a more secure limb, farther down the trunk, and looking back at the wild swirl of the foliage, with the stars dancing madly in the black sky beyond, he wondered that he ever had been foolish enough to attempt the thing at all.

He rested a moment, getting breath.

Then a great impulse swept over the heart of the boy, unavoidable and irresistible. It carried him straight up the tree, and onto the great tremulous lower branch. Then he was hanging by two lower boughs—no, twigs they should be called. One moment he swayed out over the ground a dizzy distance below. A man was lighting a cigarette. The flame which he held, cupped between his hands, streaked out in a yellow line. It was like the downward pitch of a long fall, that dangling flight, hitched to the breaking twigs of the tree. Then the roof of the barn leaped up beneath him, seeming to plunge upward.

He loosed his hold and landed by the grace of luck, flat on his back on the roof.

His wind was knocked from his body. His head rang with the force of the blow so that all the stars in the heavens spun before his eyes, and he thought of how he had stood before big Alabama Joe in terror of his life. Now he was risking that life to save the criminal!

This he thought about but did not reflect on long.

He had to be up. He had to get to Alabama Joe quickly, or else all that he had done so far would have been done in vain.

So he crawled down to the eaves to the roof and there he lay. He felt the insistent hands of the gale, worrying him, and the scream of it striking into his ears, and half drowning the voice of the orchestra.

He would be estranging himself, to be sure, from the ways of the law-abiding. Alabama Joe was hunted across and across the continent. He was famous for the distance to which he fled, like a migrating bird. He, if he threw in his lot against the mounted police, would have to lead exactly such a life. They never forgot and they never would leave his trail.

Reform school first. Then a branded, shamed, disgraced life, forcing him toward crime. He thought of Awaskees, erect, high-headed thoroughbred in all the ways of his body and of his thought. He thought of Paula Carson. These people, finally, would scorn to know him.

Just as a road lures forward the weary traveler to turn the next curve, so Jimmy was drawn on against his conscience and his better sense by the thing to which he had put his hand.

He went over that unsteady roof gutter with a lurch, hung down by his toes, and found the weight of the wind forcing him in like a hand toward the side of the barn. Then he got his grip on the ladder and was again swinging hand over hand along the narrow ledge, swearing to himself that he never would stop again for an instant's thought until the task was ended.

So went Jimmy Green to the window where he had crouched before and found the dance in full progress.

He could not wait to reach the ear of the big fellow by any stratagem. He simply called out, at once, and the Stingaree, waving back the others, who would have crowded curiously forward, got to the window instantly.

He leaned out, pulling the shutters wide enough for his head to thrust between the edges. The gale went screaming into his smiling face and past his wide shoulders. Jimmy heard the girls squeaking with dismay like flurried mice, but the sound of the orchestra came out strongly to him and seemed to draw him into the very room itself.

"Aye, Jim?" asked big Stingaree.

He was most casual. One might have thought that every night young boys risked their lives in his service, clambering in wind-broken trees for no reward, except the exquisite pleasure of serving his majesty!

And Jimmy almost smiled, when he thought of this. He cried out softly:

"I've got Awaskees. Joe, go fast! Charlie Dyce and five other Mounted Police are in this town."

The other whistled softly.

"Five more? No, no, Jim. They never send that many for one crook like Alabama Joe."

"They're here, Joe! One of them is tied and safe. The boys did for him. Two more are at the house of Parker. Dyce and another are sure to wind up at the dance soon. They think they have plenty of time. That's the only point where you may beat 'em. I've got Awaskees. Hurry!"

"I'll meet you in front in a minute," said the Stingaree. "Don't worry, old son. You and me—half the world couldn't beat us!"

He closed the shutters in Jimmy's face. No questions were asked by him about how the boy could get down from his perilous position, and once more a great doubt of this man came up in Jimmy's mind.

How could he tell that Alabama Joe, besides being a known criminal, was not now using him cunningly, carelessly, as a mere tool?

He got down to the ground as fast as he could climb, and hurried around to the door.

There he saw the tall, stately form of Awaskees in the distance. Nearer the door he saw two other shapes which startled him. It is hard for us to believe in our own prognostications. There was one of his, he felt, about to be accomplished before he had time to think.

Near the door were several men hot from dancing, now enjoying the wind which flared their forelocks above their bronzed faces. But back from the circle of light, esconced behind two trees, were another pair of waiting men. Jimmy saw the glint of the distant light on their faces and knew them. They were Henri and Simon Lafitte, the gunmen.

He wanted to run forward to the doorway and there warn the big man, but somehow he dared not bolt straight forward. Instead he circled a little, and so came up close behind Henri, who leaned against the tree trunk. Twenty yards away was the other brother, ready to take the enemy at a separate angle. They would enfilade Alabama Joe from two sides.

Jimmy had no time to form a good plan for interference.

At that very moment out of the door came the tall form and the easy step of the Stingaree. He even paused an instant, so great was his calm, to speak a word to men at the door.

They answered him with grins. Since this night not a man in Fort Anxious but would be glad to be seen speaking with this stranger, this modest man-handler. But what madness in Alabama Joe! For all he knew, Dyce and his men might be waiting there among the shadows of the trees, ready to seize him with an overmastering force of numbers.

Then, to the left, Jimmy saw Simon Lafitte move his hand, and metal gleamed in it. And a gun was raised carefully by Henri at the same moment.

"Joe! Joe!" screamed Jimmy Green. "Duck!"

Henri Lafitte whirled on him with wonderful agility and, leaping back at the boy, struck for him with the long glittering barrel of his revolver. The force of that blow would have shattered Jimmy's skull, but it would have been as easy to strike a sparrow on the wing as Jimmy prepared to dodge.

He heard Lafitte curse; and then the double crack of two revolvers exploding at almost the same instant.

CHAPTER TWENTY-FIVE

THAT FIRST SIDE-SPRING of Jimmy's was perfectly successful to elude the rush of Lafitte, but the second step tripped him on a root and he whacked the ground hard.

He was gone, he felt. And so he would have been if Henri Lafitte had not had something else on his mind.

He, swerving toward the sound of the gun shots, could see his brother tilting forward from behind the tree, not so much like a man falling as like a post toppling stiffly.

And near the doorway was the Stingaree, crouching a little, the same pencil-stroke of gun smoke streaked before him which Jimmy had noted on that first day in the meadow. With the naked weapon ready for a second attack, the Stingaree turned a little from side to side, looking among the shadows of the trees.

That was enough for Henri Lafitte. He turned on his heel and fled like the wind, while Jimmy, calling frantically—lest the other should shoot a friend by mistake—got up and hurried not toward Alabama Joe, but toward the wounded man, who now was twisting and writhing on the ground.

All the others were bent in the same direction.

The Stingaree ran in the lead. The men who had been in the doorway behind him lurched out from shelter and followed.

Jim, coming up almost shoulder and shoulder with Alabama Joe, saw what Simon Lafitte was working toward. The man had the vitality of a snake and the treacherous ferocity of a tiger.

The bullet had clipped through the thigh of one leg, and, angling down, it had plunged deeply into the knee of the other.

He was not dead. He was in no danger of dying. And his one purpose was to strike effectively at his foe before he received another shot. In falling, the revolver had dropped from his hand to a little distance. He was dragging himself toward it on his two hands, since he could not move his legs.

Crimson streamed from his wounds. His face was a set picture of wicked resolution, ghastly pale.

The wounded man actually had his hand on the gun when the Stingaree kicked the weapon free, and Simon Lafitte, turning on one elbow, stared balefully up at Alabama Joe.

"What started you on my trail?" said Alabama Joe loudly, as he leaned over the fallen man.

Lafitte snarled at him like a dog. "I'll talk to the judge about it!" said he.

"You lie. You'll speak to me, and now," said Alabama Joe.

"I'll talk to the judge," insisted Simon Lafitte. "Attack—intent to murder—that's the charge against you. Where's a policeman? Any good citizens to seize on this man?"

He snarled again.

"Here are six that saw you pull your gun from behind the tree and make the first move," warned Joe. "Is it likely that I'd stand in the light of the doorway and take a shot at you—behind a tree? Lafitte, open up and talk. Maybe I'll not stay to make witness against you!"

"You won't stay!" nodded Lafitte. "Dyce is here for you! He's likely coming now!"

He laughed. The sense of security in the future, mixed with disappointment, and the agony of his wounds made that laughter like a wild howl.

"We saw it all," said one of the witnesses. "You ought to have blown his head off, Alabama Joe! I saw you aim low.

On purpose, I'll bet. I'd have no mercy on that rat—that poisonous rat—that Lafitte!"

"I'll remember that!" said Lafitte, glaring up toward the speaker.

"Oh, remember it as long as you please," said the other. "You'll have less spirit when your blood has finished running!"

Alabama Joe kneeled by Lafitte.

"Will you talk?" he asked gently.

"Dang you, no!" burst out Lafitte.

What Alabama Joe did, Jimmy could not tell. He laid hands on the wounded fellow in some way, and a wild shriek burst from the lips of Lafitte.

As it died out, "Will you speak?" persisted Alabama Joe gently, in exactly the same voice which he had used before.

"Take him away from me!" gasped Lafitte, exhausted with terror and with excess of agony. "You brutes, will you stand by?"

They stood by!

"Again?" said Alabama Joe. "Do I have to ask you again, Lafitte?"

The latter suddenly turned limp. He lay flat on the ground. Perhaps loss of blood was telling on him, as well as fear of that same torturing stroke of pain.

"Parker!' he gasped. "He sent me!"

"You and your brother?" asked Alabama Joe.

"Me alone."

"He lies!" said Jimmy. "Henri was behind that other tree with a gun in his hand, when I yelled out to you!"

"A good job you did it, kid!" said one.

Lafitte was enough stimulated by rage and spite to raise himself upon one elbow again, and now he glared at the boy.

"You!" said he.

And he pointed at Jimmy with a crimsoned forefinger, injured by the kick of Joe which had dislodged it from the handle of the gun.

He would remember, beyond doubt, and Jimmy would as soon have been remembered by a ghost, he felt. The cold went through him and stayed shuddering in his spine.

The witnesses had huddled their heads close around the fallen man and his confession.

"Parker sent him! The yellow dog didn't have the nerve to come back and fight it out by himself," said one. "Him to kill a wild cat like Dillman in a fair fight. I tell you, boys, we've been fooled by a four-flusher. That's all that Stan Parker is!"

They growled assent. Stanley Parker had swayed them like a king; now they saw that his scepter was a lie, and they raged at the thought.

"Now, then, Parker sent you?" went on Alabama Joe.

Lafitte glowered balefully on him, but he dared not submit to the cruel grip of those hands again.

"Parker sent me," he said, the words wrung out of his twisted mouth. "Parker sent me. Dang him!"

"And Henri?"

"Yes."

He gasped out the word and glanced askance at Jimmy as he spoke.

"How much money, Lafitte?"

"I've said enough. I'll say no more, curse you!"

"How much money, Lafitte?" repeated the tramp.

"Five thousand."

"To each of you?"

"Yes, yes, yes! Dang you, is that enough said?"

"And enough paid," said the genial voice of Alabama Joe. "A good price for one murder, Lafitte. I'm honored by Parker."

Suddenly he stood up.

"Friends," he said, turning to the others, "I want to point out to you that my life has been threatened by Parker, and that he has put gunmen on my trail!"

"We'll run that man out of town!" they said.

"I'm asking you for protection," said Alabama Joe. "I'm not safe. He's tried once. He'll hire four the next time. He has all of old Tyndal's money under his thumb, and he'll spend it on me!"

"He won't have Tyndal's money longer than tomorrow morning," said one of the bystanders. "Tyndal will turn him out when he hears about this. Tyndal's as square as they come!"

"They say that Dyce is in town," said Alabama Joe. "I want to see him. I'm going to hunt for him now. I need protection, my friends. You're witness that that brute of a Parker is after my life?"

They were witnesses. Heartily they assured him.

And then, as they began to take care of the wounds of the fallen man, the Stingaree melted out of sight among the tree

103

shadows as skillfully as his namesake ever blended itself with the tanned sands of a beach.

Jimmy was at his side. Soft-stepping Awaskees was instantly with them, and pointed off in the direction of the river.

"He means that he's ready for you, Joe," interpreted the boy. "How'd you see that fellow in the dusk of the trees, Joe? How'd you manage to get out your gun so quick on him when he had the first drop?"

"Your yell was the light that I saw by," said Alabama Joe. "That got the gun out for me, and I fired at the first twinkle among the trees. It was luck that let that bullet hit poor Lafitte."

One might have thought that he really pitied the fallen man, so tender was his tone. But it was not pity, Jimmy Green knew. It was simply a vast, controlled malice. The murderous fury of a dozen like the Lafittes could never make up the cold wrath of Alabama Joe.

"We'll have to hurry, Joe!" said the boy. "We'll—"

He was suddenly caught up by the strong hands of his companion and planted at his side behind a tree.

As for Awaskees, there was no sight of him. He had vanished into the thick blue-black of the evening.

But there was something else to be seen, and it was enough to fill the eyes of Jimmy Green.

It was the natty picture of two uniformed Mounted Police marching side by side down the center of the street, with their repeating carbines over their arms. They marched in step jauntily. And Jimmy Green knew the tall form and the step of Charlie Dyce as one of the two.

CHAPTER TWENTY-SIX

THE PAIR STOPPED after they had gone half a dozen paces beyond the hiding place of Stingaree. Jimmy Green saw the faint gleam of the drawn gun in the hand of the latter, and he knew that the police lay practically in the hand of the criminal. With such speed and accuracy as he had shown, he could even call out a warning, and still drop his men before they started fighting.

He was tempted, furthermore, to take this chance, as the boy could see in the stiffening of his body and hear in the quick breathing of Alabama Joe. But the big fellow controlled himself. He was held on a leash, and the boy wondered who held the other end of the chain!

"Shall we go straight into the hall?" asked the companion of Dyce.

"Yes," said Dyce. "This Stingaree won't start shooting in a crowd where he's liable to hurt the bystanders. All the same—"

"What? Are you worried?"

"I am a little. I've split the boys up a good deal. That's not the way of Napoleon, eh?"

"Any one of us ought to be good enough to try any arrest," said the other.

"That's the theory, and a mighty fine theory—only I don't know how it'll work with the Stingaree. Mind you, Jack—if he flashes a gun, be braced to shoot. If he draws, one of us will go down. If it's me that falls, don't pay any attention to me. Go on after him."

"I will. The same goes for me, Charlie. Anything else?"

"One thing. Shoot low. He's done that much himself for others. It seems to me that he ought to get the same sort of break himself. Wing him if you can and stop him."

"That's a long chance, Charlie."

"It's the fair thing, though. He'd have fifty killings on his hands if he'd shot to kill always. But he hasn't done that."

"Too wise, eh?"

"Or too decent. I don't know. Come along, Jack. We'll dive in and try to catch this fish alive."

They went on. The dark closed behind them, opened a little, and finally they were gone.

Awaskees materialized silently beside the friends.

"The canoe is at the head of the lake," he said.

"Let it stay there a while, my friend," said Stingaree. "I have two things to do before I leave Fort Anxious."

"You ain't going to stay here, Joe?" gasped the boy.

"Only a little while. Steady, Jim, and come along with me. I need a queer sort of help for this next job. Awaskees, we'll meet you at the canoe in a little while."

The Indian said nothing. And Jimmy went on at the side of big Alabama Joe with a growing fear.

Two things still to be done, as though that night had not been filled with enough action already!

They went to the Carson store, and going back to the living quarters, the tramp lifted Jimmy so that he could look through the window. He could report that old Bill Carson sat in the room with his chair tilted back. The room was thick with pipe smoke, and Bill, as usual, was studying his paper.

So Alabama Joe led the way to the rear door and entered, for the door was unlocked. As they stepped into the presence of the grocer, he did not look up, but grunting out a cloud of smoke, he said:

"Here's a fine thing! Listen: Gent in Skagway has got two daughters. They fall in love with a pair of crooks, rope the old man, and let the crooks in to get the coin—whacha think of that, Alabama?"

"Every man loses a good deal by a daughter," said Stingaree.

Carson looked up.

"You, there, Jimmy Green, you plunderin', worthless young rascal, what trouble are you makin' here tonight?"

He looked ready to rush at the boy, but Jimmy Green merely smiled. He was sure of the strong arm of his protector.

"Just dropped in. I thought it was your birthday, maybe!" said Jimmy.

"I dunno how you can take to a brat like that," said Carson to Alabama Joe. "Worse'n a bunch of nettle and mixed barbed wire. Get out of here, Jimmy Green! What's the news, anyway?"

He grinned at the boy, and Jimmy answered promptly:

"Old Les Johnson, he's traded his gray mule and fifty dollars boot for young Dickinson's bay mare."

"Hey, hold on! That ain't a mule. That's only a skin stuffed with meanness and old age."

"Yeah," said the boy, "but he gets fifty dollars, Dick does."

"That ain't any price for a fine upstanding bay mare, like that."

"Ain't it?"

"No, old Les Johnson is a skinflint, I tell you. Confound a man like that, making things hard for boys like Dickinson!"

"That mare has gone and broke her wind," said the boy quietly. "If she so much as pulls her own weight up to the top of a hill, she'll never be able to walk down the other side.

Les Johnson is gunna do some of the finest cussing that ever we heard around Fort Anxious. I'd mighty like to be there and learn something when he busts the damn."

Bill Carson lay back in his chair and rolled like a ship in a storm. Laughter tormented him, and made him groan.

"You, Jimmy. What else is happening?"

"Well, Alabama Joe has come home early from the dance. That's one bit of news that you'd see if you was to look at the clock."

"Hey!" said the grocer. "You get tired of the dance, Joe?"

"I had to have a talk with you, Carson."

"Well, son, fire away."

"You were saying something about daughters."

"Yeah? You wanta talk about Paula? You gunna complain? Lemme tell you, son, that I've seen for a long time that you got no use for Paula, and she got none for you. All the same you gotta fight your own battles with her. Understand? I ain't able to handle her. I'd rather take giant powder and a burning fuse in my fingers than Paula when she'd made up her mind about anything. You gotta fight the thing out with her, Joe. Get up your courage, boy! But maybe things would be better right away if you didn't tease her so much."

"Tease her?" said the tramp.

"I mean, askin' her all the time how she's gunna lay out the garden at the Parker house, and that kind of thing. That gets her pretty hot. She's gunna marry Parker and—"

Alabama Joe lifted his hand.

"I've got a few minutes to talk to you, Carson," said he. "But I can give you some news. She won't marry Stan Parker."

The grocer, starting to speak and checking himself, was like a fish biting at the air.

"Whatever she does, she won't marry him," insisted Alabama Joe.

"The young fool!" shouted Carson, crashing his fist down on the table. "Has she gone and had a fight with a brace of millions on toast?"

"She won't have him. He's a yellow streak, and a murderer, Carson."

"Hey?"

"He went partners with Dillman and then double-crossed him, and that's the true story, Carson. Fort Anxious believes it. I proved it tonight."

"Proved it? You? How, man?"

"I haven't the time to tell you, Carson."

"You ain't got the time? Then you're mighty badly rushed. What you wanta tell me about, son?"

"About Paula's husband."

"Eh? What about him? You tellin' me that she's married?"

"As good as."

The door opened softly. By a sagging outward of the smoke, which flowed down from the ceiling like water, Jimmy had his attention called, and looked to find that Paula Carson herself was standing in the entrance of the room. She must have heard the last words. Her face was very pale, and her eyes wonderfully brilliant. She made to Jimmy a gesture demanding silence.

He was amazed that Alabama Joe, hair-trigger as his senses were, should not be aware that another person had entered the room. As for Carson, he was nearsighted. But the two faced one another oblivious of all else.

"Her!" exclaimed Bill Carson, staggered by this information. "Her as good as married—my Paula! Hey, young feller, what in heaven's name d'you mean?"

"I mean that the man's found her who's sure to marry her," said Alabama Joe.

"Has he? What's his name? Somebody been sneakin' around and—"

"No sneaking. But he's been seeing her morning, noon and night!"

"I'll knock him down and throw him to Mishe Mukwa!" roared Bill Carson. "What's the name of the puppy?"

"Alabama Joe," said the tramp.

CHAPTER TWENTY-SEVEN

IT WAS GOOD to see the confusion, the astonishment, and then the laughter of the grocer.

"You—you—you!" he shouted.

Alabama Joe stood smiling and nodding, as though he appreciated the joke, too.

Suddenly Carson barked: "You ain't serious, man?"

"Yes, I am," said Joe.

"Well, I'll be danged," boomed Carson. "You—Alabama Joe—"

"Tramp and all that," nodded Joe, still smiling.

"Crook, for all I know!"

"Oh, I have been, all right," said Joe. "Bank breaking, train stopping, a little in the way of sticking up stages, too, back in the hills, and a whirl at foot-padding in the towns, with a little second-story work to freshen things up—nothing like going into rooms that may hold guns on you, eh?—or let's say some plain gun fighting, now and then. A crook of all those kinds, Carson. I've rustled cows. I've even rustled sheep. I've taken a whirl at running off horses, though I didn't like that—"

"Go and tell Paula what you've done, and then ask her what she thinks!" shouted Carson.

"I've told her already," said Alabama Joe.

"And she told you to come and talk to me?"

"She told me nothing at all."

"Then what made you think—are you crazy, Alabama?"
Bill Carson half rose from his chair, as though he were going to hurl himself at the other.

"Don't attack me," said Alabama Joe. "I've got Jimmy here as a witness if you get violent."

"You low cur," yelled Bill Carson, "I dunno what you're drivin' at. You want me to kick you out of the house? Or shall I leave Paula to whip you out?"

"If she did, she'd ask me back, I think," replied Alabama Joe. "I've simply had to come here to ask your permission before I ask Paula if she'll marry me."

"Crazy? Why, crazy as a loon!" said Mr. Carson to himself. "Go on, Joe, and tell me anything more that you got on your mind! Give my daughter to you, eh? Give Paula to you?"

"I'd make her a good husband," said Alabama.

"Yeah. Juggling the teacups to keep her amused, eh?"

"I can work," said Alabama.

"At what?"

"Selling groceries, for instance," said he.

Carson snorted. "Did you seriously talk to Paula?" he asked.

"I did a little."

"Tell me what she said, and then I'll know how much remains for me."

"For you to do?" asked Alabama.

109

"Yes. Because if you've got her interested in you, I'll take your hide off in strips, I will, and toast you at the fire!"

He got up as though he intended to attack that moment, and then Jimmy, looking back at Paula, saw her step a little forward.

"Daddy," said she.

Old Carson reeled. "Hey, where'd you come from, Paula?" he cried.

"Through the door," said she. "I wanted to introduce you to Joe before you take his hide off, Daddy. He's the Stingaree."

Old Carson slumped into a chair with a force that made its legs creak.

"Stingaree!" said he, and rubbed his hand across a very wet forehead.

It was the Stingaree himself who seemed upset by Paula's coming. She went past him with a grave face and stood by the edge of the table, resting a hand upon it, and quickly rehearsed what had happened.

"It seems that Stanley Parker after all murdered Dillman. But, anyway, I'd made up my mind that I couldn't go on with him. He fought Joe, was knocked down, and went home. I've just found out the details. No one would tell me while Joe stayed at the dance. Then he hired the two Lafitte brothers to murder Joe. Joe drove them off."

"How d'you know that Parker hired them, then?"

"Because Simon was left on the ground—and Joe tortured him until he confessed."

When she came to the word "torture," she turned to Joe, and he winced visibly.

"Everything's topsy-turvy," muttered Bill Carson. "I don't understand—"

"Joe is in a hurry," said she in the same calm manner. "He's been guilty of all the crimes he's just confessed, I suppose. At least, you've heard of the Stingaree before. Everything—except murder! But when he talked to me at the dance, I found that I didn't care about what he'd done in the past, so long as he could change for the future. It's pretty square of him to come here and talk to you so frankly. Daddy, what do you advise?"

Bill Carson mopped his brow again.

"Paula," said he, "if he was an ordinary man, I wouldn't take any time. I'd tell you that I'd rather see you dead than married to him. But the Stingaree has made a name that's gone from one end of the country to the other. He's a man. He might be a bad man. But he ain't the kind that's turned out nowadays by the hundred dozen. His kind, they're made one at a time. Paula, tell me: Are you fond of him?"

"More than of anybody I've ever seen," said she.

"Fond of him, fond of him—" muttered the grocer. "Well, I guess that that answers me all right. You'll marry him, then."

"Unless he's put in prison first," said Paula, "or—is guilty of murder, Daddy!"

Big Alabama lurched toward her and then was stopped by her last words.

"There are six Mounted Police looking for him in Fort Anxious now," she went on, "but he remained here, you see, for two things. One was to talk to you. The other is to reach Stanley Parker, and kill him!"

Bill Carson could not answer. And it was the Stingaree who stepped into the breach now.

"I'm trying to understand you clearly, Paula," said he. "You'll have me if I keep my hands clean from now on?"

"Yes," said she, her voice suddenly failing her.

"Parker's a cur!" he told her with great excitement. "I've trailed him for three thousand miles. I've run him down. He belongs to me, Paula. I tell you, there would be no charge laid against me. Everybody in Fort Anxious knows that he's hired men to kill me. Everybody knows that he's probably trying to kill me now! Don't you see how simple it is? I've gone to his house to try to persuade him to give up his enmity. I've talked hard and fast to him, but he makes a sudden movement to attack me—"

His face hardened—hardened on a smile that made Jimmy Green tremble.

"Why, that's murder, Joe," said the girl.

"Not murder. Duty, honey. Duty as white as sunshine. Bob was the straightest friend that any man ever had!"

"Stanley Parker will have a dog's life. Worse than death, really!"

"Justice is justice, and if I don't take it, the law will never touch him!"

"Listen to me," broke in Bill Carson. "If you're hounded by the law, how could you give my girl a home, Joe?"

"By turning into a different man with a different name," said he. "Paula, you don't doubt that?"

"No," she answered. "I'd marry you anyway, if I knew that you had to go to prison the next minute with clean hands. No blood on them, Joe! You've fought fairly before. You couldn't make a fair fight against a broken fellow like Parker tonight."

He threw back his head with a groan. "Paula, are you tying my hands for me?"

She did not answer. And Jimmy Green knew that there was no need of an answer.

But big Alabama Joe turned on his heel and, without any other farewell than another stifled sound in his throat, ran out of the room.

Jimmy would have followed, but the girl caught him by the shoulders.

"Stay with him, Jimmy!" said she. "Stay with him and save him. Keep him from Stanley Parker, Jimmy!"

She hurriedly pushed him toward the door and Jimmy went through it staggering.

His way was as blank before him as the flat face of the night.

"Hey, Joe, Joe!" he called softly.

He had no answer.

There was not a stir, not a sound near him. And he knew then that the Stingaree was already on the way to do his work. Not even his love for the girl would stop him.

CHAPTER TWENTY-EIGHT

THERE WAS NO BRIGHT thought to come to Jimmy then.

He could think of only one possible solution, a highly dangerous and dubious one, and that was to go straight to Stanley Parker and give the man warning.

So he bolted from the grocery store, out into the roadway, and then down a twisting cow-path, and from that through a tangle of brush, and so by this very short cut he came out into the region of the bridge.

Frantically he looked up and down the street, but there was no sign of the looming shoulders of Alabama Joe.

He dashed on across the bridge. He ran with all his might. It seemed that his knees were made of lead, and that he could not possibly jerk them up fast enough in obedience to his will.

And, all the while, he saw pictures and heard sounds out of the future, and none more grisly than Stanley Parker begging for his life. Beg he would, Jimmy had seen him fall and rise again, and somehow he knew very well that the courage had melted out of the heart of the big man.

Jimmy crossed the arch of the bridge and he was speeding down the farther slope when he saw half a dozen shadows run out at him from either side.

He had forgotten that this was a night of festival for the opposing band.

Suddenly he forgot Paula Carson and the Stingaree, and Stanley Parker, who stood so near to death. He forgot them, and remembered that he was a king, who now imperiled his empire.

He could not turn back. They climbed over him in a wave, and Jimmy, turning to fight, found himself mastered and dragged to the ground. In the very excess of their shrieking triumph they lifted him again and jammed him against the rail. It was a victory to be dreamed of but not expected.

He was as a king should be. His eyes were steady as ever, and the heaving of his chest and the quivering of his nostrils were the signs of his running only.

They had various proposals, with which they filled the air. They would duck him, as a beginning. Or roll him down Saunders' Hill—also as a beginning.

"I'm done for!" said Jimmy to his heart.

But he sneered in their faces.

Then he saw a tall, long-striding form on the farther side of the bridge, and the dark silhouette of the biggest of dogs behind him. He knew that it was his friend, Alabama Joe, and that the wolf dog Mishe Mukwa was at his heels.

If he saw Joe, it was certain that the latter must see him. He yearned to cry out. But pride restrained him. If Joe cared to, his arms would soon part that heap of tangled boyhood and set him free.

But Joe went on, swiftly, softly striding, and Jimmy was left alone with his fate.

So it seemed to him. Not death, but to be beaten, shamed, dethroned. He wondered if he would be able to endure the torment without a cry.

They had decided in favor of the ducking when another boy ran up, twisted through the little crowd, and stood close to Jimmy Green.

It was Dugan.

"Jimmy," he said, "honor bright, what brung you over the bridge?"

"To fish for suckers," said Jimmy fiercely.

"Was you scouting?"

"On your night? Is it likely?" asked Jimmy scornfully. "You take me for a fool, Mickey?"

Mickey snorted with anger. But he controlled himself and his pride, answering:

"Tell me! You came across the bridge on business, Jimmy?"

And the boy at last could answer: "Aye, life-and-death business, Mickey!"

"I b'lieve you," said Mickey. "Turn and turn about. Old-timers, he goes loose!"

They wailed, they raged. But Mickey faced them down. He was not quite a king, like Jimmy, but among these lads he was at least a powerful prince. They gave way. They loosed their holds a little, and while they still were discussing, Jimmy suddenly wrenched himself free and bolted.

He had half a dozen yards head start before they could get under way, whooping.

They ran well. They ran for revenge and other urgent motives. But Jimmy was running for his life! And another life as well!

The very bitterness in his heart gave him strength. That bitterness was the calm defection of the Stingaree, and he prayed that the big man might be punished for it.

A thought of horror nerved him, too.

Why was Mishe Mukwa brought along? Was the dog to be loosed like a snarling fate at Stanley Parker?

All these things steeled him.

In a hundred yards he had gained three. In a furlong they were rapidly dropping away behind him. Jimmy Green plunged ahead, victorious and alone. The very sound of the jangling riot behind him was dying out in the distance when he turned in at the gate of the big Parker house.

He stopped there, gasping out his signal, and his two clansmen instantly were before him.

Did they know what was happening in the house?

Yes, they did. There were two Mounted Police in the

front room, playing seven-up. And in the library behind them was Stanley Parker himself, with a bruise along the side of his jaw.

Had a big man and a dog come through the gate?

No, nothing like that had come their way.

Jimmy had heard enough. He thanked and dismissed them, breathing a warning about the hostile outfit.

Then he went ahead.

He did not try to go softly or with any care. Speed was his one thought, and the promise which he had made to the girl.

He crashed the knocker against the front door.

It was opened at once, but only an inch or two, by a gloomy-faced old serving man. Jim could see that the door had been left on the chain. They were cautious in the house of Stanley Parker on this night.

"I wanta see Mr. Parker!" he gasped. He was reeling from his hot run.

"Can't," said the servant, and started closing the door.

"You one-eyed, snag-toothed, lantern-jawed nut head!" shouted Jimmy. "Lemme in, or he'll break you in two tomorrow, if he lives that long."

The servant, with an oath, unchained the door and jerked it open, for above all, he wanted to get his hands on Jimmy.

He succeeded, too, for Jimmy did not budge.

His steadiness seemed to unnerve the servant. "I oughta horsewhip you!" said he.

"You take me to your boss. You hear me talk? I mean business! Life or death is what I mean to him!"

And the other, suddenly, was convinced. He growled a threat over his shoulder, but he led the way into the house, and knocked at the library door.

"Who's there?" demanded an impatient voice from the inside.

"Me, sir."

"What you want?"

"Nothing. It's Jimmy Green that wants you."

"He wants me for no good then. He never wanted anything for good in his life, and he'll wind up on a gibbet."

Jimmy was enraged, and his shrill voice sang out:

"That ain't the way that you'll finish. The law ain't gunna have time to get its hooks into you! And that's just exactly what I've come to tell you, Parker!"

There were hasty steps, the turning of locks, and then the door to the library opened.

Big Stanley Parker loomed there. A mountain of a man was he, and Jimmy wondered that any fist had been able to topple him.

"Come in!" said Parker.

He gathered Jimmy's arm in his grip, looked anxiously up and down the hall, and growling at his servant to keep his eyes open, he took Jim into the room.

CHAPTER TWENTY-NINE

THAT LIBRARY Jimmy never was to forget. The books that filled the shelves were mostly in sets, twenty and thirty in a group all of one binding. Jimmy wondered how any one in the world could afford the time to read so many thousands and tens of thousands of pages. Rumor said that young Mr. Parker, for one, could not. But he maintained a good show.

To dress up his part of "gentleman," he was now wearing a smoking jacket and soft, loose slippers. But he wore a scowl, and Jimmy could not take his eyes from a reddish patch which was swollen out on the side of his jaw. There the fist of hard-hitting Alabama Joe had landed. It seemed to Jimmy that that blow had knocked Parker down from far more than his actual height. He had fallen from position and fortune. He was down, and Jimmy wondered if the man ever could get up again.

There was a fire burning in the biggest fireplace that Jimmy Green ever had looked at, and big Stanley Parker stood in front of this, spreading his legs widely, frowning with serious thought down at the boy, and tamping a load of tobacco into the bowl of his pipe. Then he lighted a match.

"Mr. Parker," said the boy, "I dunno—you'll think me crazy. But you better beat it! He's comin' for you!"

The lighted match went out between the fingers of Parker.

"Coming? Who's coming, boy?" he asked.

"You know mighty well!" exclaimed Jimmy Green. "Alabama Joe is coming! The Stingaree!"

The other turned pale. But he lighted another match.

"Let him come," said he.

He placed the flame over the bowl of the pipe and drew deeply on it. A cloud of smoke burst out and obscured his face. He waved a passage through it, and looked out at the boy.

"I expect him, and I've set the trap, Jimmy," said he.

Jimmy's jaw fell.

Mr. Parker, still regarding him, smiled with pitying contempt.

"You've done a good thing for Fort Anxious, Jimmy, bringing in loafers, thieves, murderers like the Stingaree. But tonight you'll have a chance to stand in on the finish of him."

Jimmy moistened his white lips.

He began to feel that he had played the part of a fool in every way, in leaving the side of the tramp and coming to warn this intended victim—a victim already armed and defended by two Mounted Police!

"One of the Northwest Mounted is enough to handle any criminal," pointed out Parker. "There are two in the next room. A strange freak of fortune made six of those fellows converge on Fort Anxious at the same time. And the whole lot of them are hunting for the Stingaree. However, Jimmy, I'd like to know what brought you here? To warn me?"

Jimmy could not answer. He was trying to visualize that trap, and the chances of Alabama Joe.

"You're sure he can't break in?" he asked breathlessly.

"Well, Jimmy, you can see for yourself," said Parker. "That big window opens onto a drop of more than fifty feet— the little canyon wall of the creek, Jimmy. Listen, and you'll be able to hear the noise of the water."

It was quite distinct. It sounded like very faint and far thunder. One could hardly notice it, until attention had been called that way.

"There's two doors," said Jimmy.

"One opens into the hall, where that old fellow stands that let you in. I'd trust that hawk even with a Stingaree in its claws. That opposite door runs into another hall which has no window and goes down to a garden door, very heavy, locked, and chained. Now, then, Jimmy Green, what are the chances of Mr. Joe Stingaree getting into my house?"

A quick tap came at the door of the library, which was instantly opened by the servant.

"Mr. Tyndal's comin'!" said he.

And the old man stepped into the room the instant after.

He did not seem to see Jimmy. His keen old eyes, under their drooping and puckering lids, were fixed on his newly appointed heir alone.

He never had been famous for courtesy or a light touch. Now he went straight to the point without any greeting:

"Stanley, what's the meanin' of this chatter that's goin' round the town?"

At the opening of the door, Parker had stepped to the desk and caught up a heavy, new revolver which was lying in an open drawer. This he dropped hastily as old Tyndal entered.

The shock of the old fellow's appearance at that moment and the greater shock of that sudden question fairly staggered Stanley Parker. He was only able to say:

"What talk, sir?"

Old Tyndal was watching the green-gray color of the other.

"What talk, sir?" he quoted with a sneer. "What talk, sir? Why, dang it all, talk that you met up with that new loafer, that tramp, that no-good jugglin' skunk that's come to Fort Anxious; and that he was insulted by you in the dance hall; and that he took you outside to fight; and that he knocked you flat; and that you got up and crawled home without hittin' back! That's a part of the talk! I wanta know the meanin'!"

He had talked long enough for Parker's wits to begin to work again.

"If a snake crossed your path, would you tackle it with your bare hands, sir?" said he.

"A man ain't a snake!" said old Tyndal.

"There's some one else here," said Parker uneasily. He motioned toward Jimmy. "And that fellow, Alabama Joe, is really the Stingaree! Bob Dillman's partner!"

"What do I care who's here?" thundered Tyndal. "I wish that the whole town was here to listen to your excuses! You stood up to Dillman, you said. Are you afraid of the Stingaree?"

The jaw of Stanley Parker sagged. He had the look of a man who has been struck violently, and who is stunned to the verge of falling to the ground.

"I'm gunna give you time," said Tyndal. "I'm gunna give you till the mornin' to make up a lie—or to kill that Stingaree like an honest fightin' man. And if there ain't something done, I'm gunna pick you as bare as a bird for boilin', and turn you loose! Mind what I say to you!"

He turned on his heel, with no more farewell than there had been greeting from him in the beginning, and the door slammed behind him.

Stanley Parker rubbed both hands upward over his face. Then he pointed at the boy.

"What are you waiting for?" he asked harshly. "Get out of the house, you and your warnings. Get out or I'll—"

Jimmy did not wait to be invited twice.

He merely said: "You keep your eyes open, Parker. It ain't what happens to you that I reckon on or care about. I don't want the Stingaree to get his hands dirty with the handlin' of you. That's all!"

He started for the door, and swung back to fire a parting shot, when a light, hissing sound took his ear. It was like a breath, sharply drawn. A paper which lay on the floor rattled harshly. And Jimmy was turned to stone.

From the door which led toward the garden that sound had come.

Parker, overwrought with the last blow which had fallen on him, seeing only his own ruin before him, had remained oblivious of the noise, but Jimmy gasped at him:

"Don't you hear it, Parker?"

The latter stared at him as though only partly comprehending.

"The garden door—it's open—and he's here!" said Jimmy.

And to re-enforce his words, there was a faint hiss of the draft again beneath the inner door.

Parker could understand that.

If he had been pale before, he was stone-white now. He said not a word, but went for the door with his hands stretched out before him, like a man fumbling through the dark, and terror on his face. Through the door into the outer hall went Parker, unable to speak.

That door closed again, and Jimmy wanted with all his soul to follow, but could not.

Just opposite him the knob of the other door was turning slowly, so slowly that he would not have been able to guess at the motion, if he had not noticed the slight shifting of the highlight on the brass.

And then the door sagged open. In the dark rectangle stood Mishe Mukwa, grinning evilly, and only dimly, behind him, appeared the shadowy bulk of the tramp.

The latter came in without sound, running half crouched, with the gun ready in his hand and murder indeed in his face.

He saw the emptiness of the room, then, except for Jimmy's frozen face at the opposite door, and he got to the boy in one bound.

"You back-stabbing little cur!" said the Stingaree, and reached at the throat of the youngster.

He checked himself at the last moment.

Out of the next room a choked voice was stammering something. It rose to a sudden scream.

"He is! He is! I tell you, he's likely in the library now! Go after him, if you're worth your salt!"

Chairs scraped noisily back. But still the tramp hesitated, and in his face a grim and desperate question worked for an instant.

"No," he said, half aloud. "Only Parker!"

He grabbed Jimmy by the shoulder.

"Get out of here with me. You've been a traitor once. I'll not give you a second chance!"

CHAPTER THIRTY

THEY WERE THROUGH the doorway into the hall which pointed toward the garden almost at once, and Stingaree waited to lock it behind him. Then he went on. The other door stood open, with a fresh, damp breeze blowing through it; and as they reached this, they heard the charge of the two Mounted Police into the library which they had just left. The two reached the inner door. The knob rattled, and then the hinges groaned as they threw their weight against it.

The Stingaree was locking the outer door behind him, now, and throwing the key aside into the garden.

"Which way, Jimmy?" he asked cheerfully.

One would have thought that nothing of moment had happened, and that there was no trouble or shadow in the mind of the man from the South.

"I'm a traitor," said Jimmy sullenly. "You better pick out your own way!"

"Traitor to me, but straight as a string with Paula Carson,

nd she's an older friend. Which way, Jimmy, before they
me out and swallow us alive?"

He dropped his hand on the big head of Mishe Mukwa as
e spoke. There was a crash inside the house. The police had
urst open the inner door, and their footfalls rushed down
e hallway.

"Are you going to take the canoe?" asked Jimmy.

"Yes."

"Then we'll go down the creek bottom. That comes out
ose to where Awaskees will be waiting."

"That's rough going—that canyon, Jim!"

"Go out the other way, then," said Jimmy. "Go out and
un straight into Charlie Dyce!"

They had gone a little distance into the thick tangle of the
arden, as they talked, and now Mishe Mukwa crouched
addenly flat against the ground. Jimmy needed no further
int. He flattened himself on the soil, likewise, and jerked at
e hand of Alabama Joe to bring him down.

The drop of the boy had been instant. That of the Sting-
ree was much slower, and he muttered: "What's up?"

"I dunno," said Jimmy. "I dunno what to make of it. Shut
p! Lie still and listen!"

For ten seconds they listened. Then, as they heard the dis-
ant, running footfalls and their odd echoes inside the house,
 voice spoke close beside them:

"I saw something out here just now, Charlie."

"Talk soft. You can't tell. He may be near—the sneaking
ur!"

Charlie Dyce was there. Dimly, Jimmy could see him rising
ut of the bushes.

"I saw something," repeated the other voice.

A door of the house slammed noisily.

A voice broke out into the open, shouting: "Dyce, Dyce!"

"Don't answer!" cautioned Dyce quietly. "Where did you
ee it?"

"There—"

Two shadows came toward the spot where the boy, man,
and dog were crouching.

The youngster did not wait. He merely whispered to Alabama Joe: "We gotta run for it. Foller me!"

Then he was up and running.

A voice barked behind them like an angry dog.

"Who's there? Halt!"

Instantly afterward a gun cracked, and Jimmy heard the snapping of the bullet through the twigs near him.

He ran like a dodging teal, winging down the wind, dodging every other step. Behind him came Alabama Joe, making wonderful speed, but held back by the swinging branches under which the boy ducked.

Half a dozen bullets in rapidly chattering succession were fired after them, and then the chase was launched. One of those bullets, Jimmy could have sworn, had parted his hair for him. But he was untouched, and he heard the grunting of Alabama close behind—grunts of effort, not of pain.

It was a wild tangle, that undeveloped garden in the midst of the woods. But Jimmy knew it, and he knew that ahead of him there was a steep and narrow path which angled down the precipitous bank of the creek's canyon wall. It was not an easy descent even in broad daylight. But still he did not hesitate. There was no other way for him to get the big man out of the danger.

For, well behind them, he heard the sound of the pursuit. There was hardly an Indian who was a better woodsman than Charlie Dyce. Certainly he had, as the saying was, eyes in his feet, and would soon overtake the Southlander in such going as this. Then it would be death for one of the two.

So the boy dropped back beside the tramp.

"Hard path—drops down creek wall—foller me close!" he gasped, and the next instant, leaping ahead, he had found the precarious descent and was plunging down it.

It was even steeper than he had remembered. And in the darkness he felt himself tripping and lurching forward with great steps, which he had to arrest by tearing at the bushes in going past.

Then he saw the pale glimmer of the water beneath him.

The wild dog had run out in the lead when Jimmy heard the grunting voice of Alabama Joe exclaiming behind him:

"Look out!"

He had stumbled with a crash through a bush that stood in the path, and now Alabama Joe leaped forward with all his might.

The great dark body shot past the boy. It was that leap for the water, or else a floundering fall which, down that slope, was sure to cost broken bones.

Down went the big man. He hit the water with a noise

like a great boulder, and the upward-flying spray struck cold on the face of the boy.

He reached the edge of the pool, and there stood the Stingaree, soaked, dark with wet, dripping into the face of the water—and making no move whatsoever to leave it.

"Are you hurt, Joe?" breathed the boy.

There was no answer.

Hurried, eager voices spoke above them.

"They went down into the canyon. What is the way?"

"I dunno. Show a light. It's in here, somewhere."

Those voices above were appallingly close, but more dreadful to Jimmy was the sight of the big man standing motionless, his head and shoulders bent.

The boy caught him by the arm and tugged on him. The whole body gave loosely. And he knew that the Stingaree had been badly hurt in the fall. Incapacitated definitely, perhaps, or at least stunned.

Yet, Jimmy did not entirely despair. He set his teeth, and pulling one big, limp arm over his shoulder, he strained to urge Alabama Joe out of the water.

He obeyed, loosely, swaying and staggering, and his long breaths sounded at the very ear of the boy.

"Steady! Steady!" Jimmy found himself whispering to the tramp. "We're gunna pull through, Alabama! Pull yourself together. Fight, Joe, fight!"

"Fight!" said the other in a faint whisper. "Fight, Stingaree! You're down!"

They were clear of the water. But the bank on which they walked was precarious going, every moment threatening to drop them both into the rocky bed of the stream again.

They left the pool. They reached the rapids. And then Jimmy Green felt the arm that hung over his neck and shoulder begin to stiffen and harden a little. The weight which had been oppressing him was lightened.

"Where am I?" he heard the big man muttering.

As if to answer him, the voice of Charlie Dyce yelled loudly from the bank above him, and behind:

"Scatter up and down the creek. I'm going down."

"Don't go, Charlie! He's down there waiting for you. We'll bag him in the daylight. He can't go far. He's smashed up. I heard the fall. Like a stone!"

"I'm going down," said Charlie Dyce. "Will you come along, Jack?"

"To the end, if you say so, Charlie—but it's a fool play, I tell you!"

"Dyce, Dyce!" said the voice of big Alabama Joe, now strong again. "If we meet, he and I—"

He let that sentence go unended. But he pulled back and halted.

Jimmy wrenched at Joe's arm.

"Are you crazy, Joe?" he pleaded. "D'you want to kill him for absolutely nothing?"

"I never crossed him. He's after me for sport. He's hunting me like a rabbit!"

"Joe, come along. He's only doing his duty. Paula—what'd she think? What'd she do if you dropped Charlie Dyce? He's the whitest in the world—Joe, come on with me!"

"The kid's right," said Alabama Joe through his teeth. "Come on, then. But where?"

"Straight down the creek. Walk soft. Keep close to me. Watch where my feet fall. Don't make a sound."

He went on, picking his way with care. Above them, on the high bank, he could hear the searchers moving, and behind, there was the noise of Charlie Dyce and his friend, lurching down the wall of the little ravine. Jimmy could hear them plunging along through the brush, as they gained the waterside.

Just above them, now, he could see the black wall of Parker's house, rising like a lofty fortress. And Jimmy went on more rapidly. Would they be cut off before they gained the edge of the lake?

Then they came out to the point where the canyon walls fanned wide apart, and before them lay the waters of the lake like tarnished silver, with a dim silhouette of a canoe upon it, and a still dimmer shadow of the craft floating alongside. It was Awaskees, at last!

CHAPTER THIRTY-ONE

BY THE TIME they came to the water's edge, the canoe was there, driven powerfully forward by the strokes of that master canoe man, Awaskees. He was more clearly seen each moment, for a pale fire seemed to be rising among the trees to the east of the lake, and Jimmy Green knew that the moon was about to rise. There was a small mound in the center of the canoe, which was a larger boat than the boy had expected to see, and as Awaskees held the craft just off the shore, he said quietly, in the Cree tongue:

"This man cannot paddle. Take the bow, brother. There is a light paddle there for you. We shall need speed. There are other boats on the water tonight."

"I'm staying in Fort Anxious," said Jimmy.

"You can return," said the Cree, "after we are into the mouth of the river and heading south."

Jimmy asked no more questions. He was already in the bow of the boat, and looking back impatiently, he saw that Alabama Joe was not with them. He was actually wasting the priceless seconds by kneeling on the narrow beach, his arms around the neck of the great wolf dog.

"Can I take Mishe also?" asked Alabama Joe.

Jimmy gasped with amazement.

It seemed to him that at any moment the enemy might break out from the woods along the shore, and in an instant the boatmen would be riddled; and yet the tramp still lingered on the shore!

"Joe, Joe!" gasped the boy. "They'll be coming. They're coming now!"

He did not need to speak twice, for back among the trees there was the distinct popping of a twig as though under the weight of a heavy foot.

Alabama Joe, at this, stood up and stepped into the water. Even then he paused to look back where Mishe Mukwa stood motionless upon the shore.

Then the tramp stepped into the canoe. That entering of the boat, alone, was enough to show that he was even less waterman than forester! He almost capsized the slender craft, and then looked around him for a paddle.

"Sit down—lie down!" commanded Awaskees.

And he began to give short, powerful strokes with his paddle to get the boat under way, though never lifting the paddle blade out of the water.

Jimmy, in the bow, was working away with a will and with a similar technique. Awaskees for many years had been training him in this fine art, and though he never could have the Indian's shadowy step upon the trail, or his matchless ear and eye in the woods, yet in the handicraft of swaying a paddle and working it noiselessly in the water, he was almost the peer of the Cree.

He began to swing the paddle with a strong, rapid stroke, and as Awaskees fell smoothly into the same rhythm, the canoe gathered speed like a horse leaving the mark. There was not a sound from the paddles, but the little waves of the lake splashed softly against the bow and went down the sides with a whispering ripple.

Except for the stillness of the water, the lake here was like a river—a winding, narrow body which twisted here and there among the trees. In a moment they were around the first bend, and an instant later they heard the voices of the pursuit breaking out from the trees behind them.

Jimmy looked back. There was no one in sight and the men of the law were well fenced away by the projecting bank. But Awaskees nodded his head toward the wake they left behind them. The boy understood. The sight of that would be as handwriting for such a waterman as Charlie Dyce to read.

Awaskees had forbidden the efforts of the tramp to take the third paddle in the boat, but now he gave the word. Silence was not needed so much as speed! And instantly Jimmy heard the splash of a clumsy paddle blade and felt the canoe jerked by the powerful thrust of the novice.

He gave directions over his shoulder, not turning.

"Keep your lower hand like an oarlock, Joe. Don't move it more than you have to. Put your weight on the upper hand. Swing your body with your stroke. Swing, swing, swing! Easily does it—easily does it!"

He talked in rhythm with his own strokes, and felt the clumsy new hand behind him smoothing his strokes in accordance. There were brains in the big man. Above all, there was the most exquisitely sensitive accord of nerve and muscle. In three weeks he could become more of a woodsman and paddler than the inept in three years. They were making famous headway, the Indian at the stern applying his strokes so nicely that there was never a waver of the bow from the straight line of their course, in spite of the unbalanced weight of two paddles against one, which is the curse of a three-man crew.

Suddenly, Alabama Joe stopped paddling.

"Stop the canoe!" he commanded.

Jimmy looked back, dismayed.

And there, in the water far behind them, already silvering

with the first pale light of the moon, he saw a small, dark object, with a wake spreading softly out to either side.

"It's Mishe Mukwa," said Alabama Joe. "I guessed that he'd follow. It's Mishe, and now I've got to take him along."

"If we stop," said the Indian, "they have a chance to get to the foot of the lake before us, and that will turn us back. Two fast miles, now, will save us a hundred later on!"

"Let the miles be hanged!" declared Joe. "I've got to have him. Shall I go on and let him drown?"

"D'you hear, Joe?" pleaded the boy. "If they cut us off at the mouth of the river, where it leaves the lake, you won't have a chance to get away. They'll turn you back into the woods, and in the woods, you're a goner!"

"I take my chance!" answered the other grimly. "The dog has to come. I knew it, back there on the beach!"

"It may be wise," said the Indian quietly. "One has to die. The dog, perhaps?"

And turning in the canoe, he began to paddle back toward the swimming dog.

"One has to die? One has to die?" muttered Alabama Joe. "What does that mean, Jimmy?"

"That's his lingo, and he'll stick to it," said the boy. "He made medicine, before he would come on this trip, and the medicine said that if he went along, somebody would have to die."

"Rot!" grunted the Southerner.

"It's what he thinks. It took a hard pull to get him started on this job, Joe!"

"Aye," said the big fellow. "I can guess that. But he's strong as a trap, once he's laid hold on a bit of work. I'll trust that man, Jimmy!"

This conversation they exchanged in soft whispers as the canoe slid back to the wolf dog which, as they came nearer, began to swim higher in the water, raising its head expectantly.

The Cree gave the signal for stopping headway. Jimmy backed water, and saw Awaskees, with miraculous skill and strength, take that ponderous new burden over the heel of the canoe—a hundred and sixty pounds of husky, loaded with another twenty pounds of wetness in his fur. But there stood big Mishe in the center of the boat trying to lick the face of his master, and with the first shake of his body showering them all with a high-flung spray.

"Get him low!" ordered Awaskees.

And at a word from Joe, the big dog sank flat, and now they started again down the lake. But Jimmy knew that with the very first stroke he could feel the leaden difference which the new weight made. They not only had lost precious time, but, furthermore, they had taken on board a heavy extra burden. He began to despair.

"Joe, Joe!" he said over his shoulder. "We're going to lose—on account of a dog!"

"A dog's not a dog when he's willing to die for you," answered Alabama, breathing the words out hard as he drove his immense power against the paddle.

Now, following the still water along the shore which, though giving them a winding course, was worth while on account of the escape from the wind riffles on the open way, they drove along with a speed which actually increased, instead of diminishing. The answer was that they were becoming attuned to one another, and their new man was picking up some of the essential elements of the craft.

He made one unpleasant suggestion.

"There's a rifle here in the bottom of the canoe, Jimmy. But after this kind of work, my hands'll be shaking so that I can't hit the side of a barn."

And Jimmy snapped: "I'd rather have you miss, if you're shooting at a man!"

Awaskees, far in the stern, heard, and commented softly: "No man will miss, if he wants enough to hit the mark."

"True," said the tramp, with an oath. "Nobody misses if he's keen enough to shoot straight!"

"How far to the mouth of the river?" he asked again, a little later.

"Another mile."

"Faster!" called Awaskees from the stern.

"We can't go faster," answered Jimmy.

"We have to," said the Cree quietly, "or else we die on this lake. Look behind!"

Jimmy jerked his head around, and he saw behind them, printed black and bold against the silver, moonlit water, a long canoe, driven forward by the powerful swaying of four paddlers and flying straight down their wake.

CHAPTER THIRTY-TWO

THEY THOUGHT that they were working at full power before. But this was a spur in the side that made them strain harder, and the trees on the bank began to brush past them at an increasing speed, except when Alabama Joe, now and then, caught his paddle clumsily in the water, slowing them.

But he was learning, studying the proper movements in even this time of desperate need.

Jimmy called over his shoulder in a last hope:

"Are they Indians or voyageurs, Awaskees?"

"White men," answered the Cree quietly.

He could tell by the paddle work in the other craft, even at that distance. And Jimmy gave up hope. Such a heavily manned craft was not apt to be out on the water at that speed and at that hour except for some such purpose as the overtaking of fugitives.

He himself was driving himself against the paddle handle until the blood rushed up into his head, and his ears hummed with the effort. His shoulders were growing numb. He could make more than thirty strokes on a side before changing. Then twenty-five. Then twenty, and he had to flash the paddle across.

When Jimmy flung a frightened glance over his shoulder again, he saw that the pursuit was gaining on them perceptibly. And yet Awaskees had never lost the wonderful pendular swing of his paddling stroke. No one, to watch him, could have guessed that he was straining the very strings of his heart. But Jimmy alone knew the secret sign. It was a thoughtful little canting of the head to one side, as though Awaskees were contemplating some distant, abstruse problem. But the instant that his head inclined from the erect, Jimmy well knew, by long experience, that the Cree was half dead from exhaustion.

"Do we take to the bank, Awaskees?" he gasped.

The Indian did not answer, and Jimmy did not repeat his question; for he knew, now, that the Cree was not willing to waste even the breath needed for a single syllable.

All three of them were desperately tired. But yet they

worked with such nerve that the canoe seemed to shoot along as rapidly as ever. They could not match four skillful paddles, however, with only two and a half—and despite his enormous power, the big man was only as half a paddle in the canoe. More men can lift their weight than can paddle it, and with both Alabama Joe and the dog in the canoe, the hands of Awaskees and the boy were filled with lead.

"It's no go. They're catching us!" said Alabama suddenly.

At that moment, the bank turned off to the right; but the Cree, instead of following the embankment, actually swung out into the open water, though the wind presently struck them, and the sharp-faced little riffles whacked rapidly against the thin sides of the boat.

Jimmy thought that the Indian had gone mad.

He threw a wild glance backward, and as they forged ahead, he saw the pursuers triumphantly cut in between them and the shore.

They were isolated on the broad breast of the lake, which had widened greatly. They could not cut back to the shore, now, and their only hope of escape would be to drive on for the mouth of the river, toward which the Cree had pointed the bow.

Half groaning, Jimmy still stuck manfully to his paddle. Defeat would be death, perhaps, for Alabama Joe. He looked back again. To his utter amazement, the pursuers had lost ground, decidedly!

He could not understand, but staring at them, while he still swung manfully at the paddle, he strove to detect some faltering of their rhythm. He could make out none. It seemed as though all the four nodded with the same swift and perfect rhythm which he had noticed in the beginning of the race. Charlie Dyce, he would dare swear, was one of that crew, and even if the others were not all Mounted Police, they were probably picked men.

One silhouette, even in the distance, the boy thought that he recognized—No. 2 man, extraordinarily thick across the shoulders, bareheaded, swaying his head sharply down at the conclusion of each mighty stroke.

It was a mannerism which he recognized, he thought, and he suddenly could have sworn that that man was big Stanley Parker.

But what explained the mystery of the defeat of such strong and practiced paddlers as those who pursued?

Suddenly the solution came to him.

It was the current, of course. What else could it be?

No white man ever had understood the changing current of that lake, depending as they did upon the wind, the height of the water, and twenty other conditions. And certainly for his own part he never had been aware of a current setting off that point for the mouth of the river.

Behind him, he heard the gasping, broken voice of Awaskees.

"Steady, brother, steady! They are beaten!"

Jimmy, looking far back, saw that two of the pursuers actually had stopped paddling and sat humped far over in their places, exhausted by that desperately long sprint. Only the steersman and No. 2 kept on their work, though with a leisurely stroke which told that they were resigned to defeat. And with this new and more leisurely examination, Jimmy was certain that No. 2 actually was Stanley Parker.

He was paddling more easily, now, hardly more than half as many strokes to the minute. It seemed as though they were resting on the paddles. The dreadful aching numbness was carried from his arms and shoulders, and the pain departed from the back of his neck. In another moment, they should be enjoying the smooth thrust and glide of the light canoe through the waters of the lake.

"I think that that's Stanley Parker in the canoe behind us, Joe," said he.

He could feel the jerk with which Alabama Joe turned his head to stare.

"It is!" said the Stingaree. "The second man?"

"Aye," said Jimmy. "How'd you guess that?"

"I've got the look of him drawn in my heart!" said the other. "I've got it there for the sake of Bob Dillman."

Then he added, after a moment: "I'll tell you something. I think that Fate wouldn't take me away from him without giving me a second chance at him!"

"What does Fate owe you?" asked Jimmy.

"A square deal," said the tramp, still breathing hard, and having to shift his paddle from time to time, yet gradually relaxing. "A square deal is all. I don't expect help when I'm robbing a bank, Jimmy," he went on, chuckling. "That's my own business. But you don't write a man off the list because he's weak in one thing. Many a good boxer is no good with a gun, Jimmy. And suppose I balance up my account and say:

131

'Well, I've robbed some banks, stuck up stages, punched heads, broken noses, and done a good many other things. But I've never done murder, Jimmy. I've had murder held out to me on a silver tray. Easy murder, rich murder, profitable murder. But there's no score against me there, Jim!' "

"Everybody go to heaven," asked Jimmy, "that doesn't do a murder?"

And he laughed, his voice shrill with relief as the chase ended, and because he could now feel the current, like a hand, taking the boat.

"Not everybody," said the yegg quietly. Then he laughed a little in turn. "I don't ask for heaven, but only for a square deal. What's murder to most? Scares them frosty to even think of it. But it's been in my line and in my way. Well, that's on record, Jimmy, my boy, and don't you forget it!"

He laughed again, and Jimmy nodded to himself. He had never marked anything like naivety in this man before. Now it stood plainly to be seen, and Jimmy was openly amazed.

They went on, now, without further speech. There was nothing to worry them until they reached the bottom of the lake. Then they would find out whether or not a message had been rushed overland to head them off. But Jimmy felt little fear of this, for they had made excellent time, except for the delay to pick up Mishe Mukwa. For his own part, he now was glad of that episode. It had showed him that the tramp was willing to risk his life for the sake of a dumb beast. Who else did he know, capable of the same effort?

Not one! Not even Awaskees, manifold as his virtues were. There was a certain cold logic which possessed most humans at such a time, and this logic the tramp was without.

He moved, it appeared, according to a certain closed code. He might die, but far rather die than violate the code.

While the boy was thinking of this, half dreamily, he heard Awaskees give the Cree soft call for caution.

Before them lay the dark mouth of the river, and he could hear the dimly musical chattering of the rapids beyond. Once in their grip, it would take a galloping horse to keep pace with them along the rough shore!

But, in the meantime, they had to pass that river's mouth, which to Jimmy began to gape like a cannon at them.

"Left! Left!" called the Cree suddenly. "For your life, brother!"

Frantically, Jimmy shifted his paddle to the right of the bow, and tugged with all his might.

Inshore he saw only one thing, but that one thing was enough. It was the flash of the moon on a wet paddle blade under the shadows of the trees!

CHAPTER THIRTY-THREE

THEY HAD COME to the lion. They almost had rowed into his mouth. And Jimmy heard, distinctly, the challenge in the name of the law, and the invitation to surrender. This was followed by a veritable volley, which broke the paddle in his grip and lanced the palm of his hand with a great splinter.

He looked down helplessly at the injured palm. Crimson was spurting there. But the main thing was that he was now useless in the boat, a mere dead weight for them to carry along.

He turned and called the information to the other two. They did not so much as answer, but bent on at their labor. The Indian's head was erect again. He had stripped off his shirt, and the moonshine glittered on his muscular torso as he swayed at the paddle. But Alabama Joe's lips grinned back from his teeth, and his eyes narrowed to points.

But they had to pull across the strong current, which distinctly tilted the canoe, and in addition to this, the ragged paddling of the novice made it doubly hard for the Indian to keep the craft into its true straight line.

They had not a chance, Jimmy decided.

Certainly, Dyce had been able to send out word in plenty of time, for here was a six-paddle canoe, with an extra rifleman in the prow to shout commands. Those six paddles were now straining in the water, and the long boat leaped away under the impetus. Firing had stopped. There was no need for that when with a few strokes they were sure to run down the pursued.

So Jimmy saw, as he looked back, and he wondered at the gravity with which his two grown-up companions continued to labor. They were lost. It seemed more graceful, and far more dignified, to simply surrender at once.

They could see the sweep of the dark hands, the lunging

of the head, and the silver-bright flashing of the naked paddle blades, reaching forward. Why struggle against such odds?

As he thought this, Jimmy saw the big canoe suddenly leap half its length from the water and land with a loud splash on the surface, beyond the submerged spit of bough over which they had ridden.

Two or three of the men were thrown from their place. Distinctly, Jimmy saw at least a pair of rifles fall into the water of the lake, and those who remained in the boat were in great confusion, some bailing, others drawing in their ducked companions over the sides of the canoe.

Only the man in the bow retained his presence of mind—and his malice. He raised his rifle and opened a rapid fire upon the fugitives. But not a shot came near them. Only chance could make one of those bullets hit the mark when the rifleman kneeled in the prow of that canoe, which reeled and rocked with the movements of the rest of the crew.

"Shall we turn back and rush for the river mouth?" asked Jimmy.

"Too late!" said the Cree.

And he was right, for along the southern shore, coming suddenly out of the moon mist toward the river mouth, Jimmy could see their first pursuers, who seemed to have been spurred on—by the noise of the firing, perhaps—and were now lifting their craft through the water at a good clip.

To Jimmy Green it seemed that the end had merely been postponed. To row back up the lake was simply to run into a hundred hands at Fort Anxious. And the passage to the south down the river was definitely blocked.

No word came from Awaskees, neither did he slacken his pace in paddling; but now he turned the canoe under the leaning shadows at the edge of the water, and presently sent the bow into the soft sand.

"Out, out!" said he. "Here we make portage!"

Jimmy had tied a rag around his hurt hand. He jumped into the water and helped as best he could while they ran the canoe on shore.

"What can I do?" he asked. "Portage to what, Awaskees?"

"Across to the first water that runs north!" said the Cree.

Jimmy gasped. Across the rough wilderness to carry a canoe, with the enemy hurrying behind them, seemed utter madness to him; but he dared not doubt the wisdom of the redman.

"Get a pack on Mishe Mukwa!" snapped Awaskees in guttural Cree. "Then follow!"

He turned the canoe as he spoke, and showed the tramp how to handle the rear end of it.

Jimmy, in the meantime, was frantically busy. The bundle in the bottom of the canoe had been arranged for a pack, and he worked with fingers that stumbled with haste. His wounded hand was burning hot and swelling already, but he made the fingers help.

And, outside the low-hanging branches, he saw the sliding outline of the canoe and its four paddlers.

"In here!" said the voice of Charlie Dyce. "They went in here!"

"Not here! Not here!" answered Stanley Parker frantically. "I tell you, I marked the place where they went ashore by that group of white birches. Go ahead!"

The paddles dipped and the craft shot on, while Jimmy, his knees weak, stood up and let Mishe Mukwa jump ahead on the trail of his master.

The dog carried the pack lightly, and Jimmy hurried up to give his strength to the carrying of the canoe.

No one but the Cree, he was sure, could find a way through that thicket; and even Awaskees was troubled by the density of the growth.

They had an eight-mile trek, winding to and fro among the trees. They spent five hours of exhausting labor to cover that distance up hill and down, until, at last, they came out of the forest gloom and saw at their feet the bright promise of a little runlet of water.

It was not by any means big enough to float a canoe, even. But they had had at least a way cleared of bush by the work of the meager water, and presently another runlet joined it.

Gasping, reeling, they went on, the water sometimes up to their ankles, sometimes to their knees. Rocks cropped up. It was a miserable, stumbling progress; but better than forcing through the trees. The lightness of the canoe alone had made their march possible. It was of Awaskees' own manufacture, and, therefore, it was perfection of best yellow-birch bark, free from the slightest wrinkle, and rich with the resin which turns the edge of the water. It was ribbed with thin strips of white cedar, powerful as whalebone, and slatted down its length with the same material. Not an ounce of extra weight was in it, and not a shade less strength than was needed for white water.

No one spoke about the enemy, but Jimmy turned the possibilities in his mind. It might well be that Charlie Dyce had guessed at their plan and had cut in ahead of them to watch the watercourses. There were several of these running through this wooded section. It only depended on his ability to select the right one.

The water now was very broken, but the rocks that projected through it like sharks' teeth were fewer, and the Cree halted. They launched the canoe, settled the pack in it, and the two men stepped aboard, with Mishe Mukwa in the center of the craft.

"You?" asked the Cree.

"I got a bad hand. I won't be much good on a paddle," said the boy. "But I hate to quit you, Awaskees—and you, Joe!"

"Go back!" said Alabama Joe. "You've done more than ten men for me, Jimmy, and I'll never forget. You're not seeing me for the last time, I can tell you! Jimmy, here's a hand, and heaven bless you, son!"

But Awaskees said not a word.

"Shall I go back?" asked Jimmy of the Indian.

"Go back and grow to be a man," said the Cree coldly.

Jimmy asked no more. He stepped into the canoe.

"No, no, Jim!" protested the white man in the bow.

But the Cree said not a word, and Jimmy accepted his fate. He had started, as it were, on a war trail, and it was better to die than to turn back.

Now the paddles dipped.

"I've gotta stay," the boy explained to Alabama Joe. "Go on! I'll manage to lift my weight, somehow!"

"True-blue Jimmy!" said the yegg. "We surely carry luck when we carry you!"

They shot down the stream. The current took them. It was constant hard paddling, now, not so much to increase the headway as to keep the boat straight on its course, or swing it around a bend with, perhaps, the current hanging straight at the farther bank. The moon stood in the zenith. The water roared in their ears. Steadily the stream increased in size, and now it lost some of the fury of its impetus.

For a good hour or so they swung along, now with only

he laziest paddle strokes, when, turning the sweep of a big
bend, Jimmy saw the blink of the moon on a straight rifle
barrel on the farther shore.

He looked again, holding his breath, and then he could
count in the shadows four dim figures of men, each with a
rifle in his hands. He himself instinctively gripped the
weapon in the bottom of the canoe, and felt the watchful
Cree nose the craft closer under the overhanging shadows of
the trees.

CHAPTER THIRTY-FOUR

WITH SUCH KEEN-EYED danger opposite them, it seemed to
Jimmy that they were rushing along at a terrific rate, and
that the men of the law must surely see them and their
dashing bow wave. But momently the pace slackened, and
now under the dark of the trees they barely crawled. Un-
warned by the Cree, the boy knew enough to jab Alabama
Joe in the back and signal to him to remain silent. Both
he and the tramp sank into the bottom of the canoe, and
Jimmy pulled down the big dog with him. Nothing now
showed above the rim of the canoe except the erect body of
Awaskees himself as with silent paddle he let the boat
drift.

Out, out, out along the point they edged, and the succes-
sive trees dipped their branches with a whisper toward the
face of the boy, as he lay there on his back frightened,
waiting each instant for the sound of the guns.

Then he felt that the canoe had turned the corner. Yes, it
was turning to the right now, and traveling each instant
farther away from danger.

Thanksgivings were forming on his lips, and instinctively
deep in his throat, when the moon blazed suddenly full down
upon him. They had come to a section where not a vestige of
a tree lined the banks. It was a freak of the soil which
would not support a shrub, even, at this spot, and they lay
naked under the eyes of their enemies.

"Who goes there? Halt!" shouted Charlie Dyce like a
sentinel.

They hardly waited for answer, but a rifle bullet came

with such a good aim that it went *clip-clip* through the sides of the canoe just over the breast of Jimmy, and he felt a chip flicker into his face.

Alabama Joe, without an instant's delay, with the courage of a very brave man, instantly was on his knees, again, and bending the paddle with his furious, noisy strokes, which set the head of the canoe bobbing like a high wind.

Jimmy, propping himself up on one elbow—there was no purpose in showing all his body—saw that two of the four had dropped to their knees, and a fourth one—that looked like Stanley Parker—was lying flat, hugging the rifle butt into his shoulder.

Four good riflemen, with a bright moon to show them a target, and the Cree—apparently gone mad—shouting: "Left! Left!"

Straight out into the open current?

Yes, and across it, the light craft dodging like a deer, and then shooting forward with wonderful speed as the current yanked it by the nose.

Nothing baffles the best of marksmen more than a change of pace, unless it be treacherous moonlight itself. Even the frantic paddling of the tramp, jerking them from side to side, was now of value, since it kept them dodging.

But what a rain of lead! Several times bullets went through the canoe. A double jet of water spurted furiously right on Jimmy's body, and he began to bail with all his might.

Then there was a cessation of paddling. He looked back. A jutting point of rocks loomed between them and the riflemen, whose fire ceased at the same instant.

They would run to take up a new position, beyond a doubt, but in the meantime an eight-knot current was sweeping the canoe forward, along a rapidly winding course, and it would be strange if the best speed of those four over broken ground could get them within range of their target again.

A few paddle strokes, now and then, kept the boat flying, and only once was there a solitary shot.

"Are you hurt, Awaskees?" shouted the tramp, turning in the bow.

"Not hurt," said the Cree.

"Jimmy, boy?"

"No," said Jimmy.

"You're our luck!" cried Alabama Joe happily. "I know

that we had our luck aboard, and they'll never put a hand on us!"

He began to sing a song on this theme, still laughing, and still swaying the paddle with an infrequent but powerful stroke. The trees sped by in a blending mass on either side. And so the moon sank, and the dimness of the night settled around them.

"Keep a sharp lookout, Joe!" called the boy, straining his own eyes ahead.

But no eye could have seen what gripped them. It was "black" water—that is, one of those sudden and furious slides when the current slopes noiselessly and with terrific speed over a smooth drop of stones. So it did now. The pull of the current caught them with a wrench that pulled their head to the right, and they were flung forward like a stone from a strong hand. The wind cut at them in a gale. Twice they staggered, gunwale deep, shipping water. As they straightened out again in quieter water beyond, Jimmy was busy bailing.

Two streams joined them, here. A slower current rolled beyond with the unmistakable surface of deep water; and the Indian kept them fairly in the center of the stream. So the dawn came over them, pink and still; and the great Northern wilderness gathered them deeper and deeper in its arms. Fort Anxious was one long day's journey behind, but it seemed to Jimmy a lifetime away.

Sometimes he looked back with troubled wonder at the Cree, unable to explain how he had come to leave the Fort, and the wife and the child who lived there. Nothing had been said to him about pay. He could be sure of nothing but great danger.

Still, he drove the canoe onward with steady strokes of the paddle. The tramp, in the meantime, kept to his share of the work, but there was a twisting lurch about his strokes that showed utter exhaustion.

When the Cree stopped the canoe under the shelter of overhanging boughs and announced that they would halt here, Joe dropped on his back upon the bank, groaning deeply.

The big dog, Mishe Mukwa, stood over him and licked the palms of his hands.

They were a dreadful sight.

Soft as the hands of a woman, almost, the first few mo-

139

ments of this unaccustomed work must have blistered them. Then the blisters broke, and the skin gradually wore off the blistered places, leaving raw flesh, which in turn would be worn away by the relentless labor of the Stingaree.

The Cree pointed down at those crimson, swollen hands. "On one leg," said he, "we only hop and crawl."

He meant that his own paddle was the only one which would be able to work the canoe forward the next day, and Jimmy agreed in silence. For his injured hand was already quite badly swollen.

They worked, first drawing up the canoe, and then, with a growing sense of disaster before him, Jimmy helped to gather materials for a fire. The teapot was brought out. From the rotten, very old wood which Jimmy had found arose hardly a trace of smoke, and this was dissipated among the trees before it rose against the sky. There was little chance that such a smoke might betray them to their enemies. And in the meantime the water boiled, the tea was made.

Strong, hot tea, bitter and black, such as the Northern travelers drink. They drank it, the hands of Alabama Joe shaking violently, though he gripped the tin cup with both. Still he drank, and drank, and then lay down on the bank again and slept instantly, while the other two ate.

"We'd better make him eat," suggested Jimmy.

"The belly will take care of itself," said the Cree.

He leaned over the sleeper and cried out softly, like a delighted child:

"Hai, Jimmy, see! What a chest! What shoulders! What a pair of arms! No wonder that he struck down Stanley Parker as a grizzly strikes down a deer! There is hard strength in the body of Parker. It is hard as oak. But soft strength is better and stronger still. Hai! See his hands! They are worn almost to the bone, but he will feel better when he wakes."

From the very shrubs that grew here, along the bank, he picked some of the smallest budding leaves, stripped off the bark of the same bush, and with the inner part of this and with the buds, he made a stew in the last water which had been heated. This he steeped for some time, and with it made a good thick poultice on each hand of the sufferer.

The latter did not waken! It was wonderful that he could sleep when those tormented hands of his were being touched.

"But if a stranger spoke a hundred steps away, he would leap to his feet," said the Cree. "This, brother, is a man!"

With all his heart, Jimmy agreed.

And it was a wonderful thing to hear the faint groans of Alabama Joe decrease and then diminish as he drew each breath to utter silence. Both hands were bandaged. And then Awaskees turned to the boy.

It was a different dressing which he prepared for him, but its touch was as magic, apparently, as that which had drawn the torment from the wounds of Alabama Joe. For the pain gradually left him. He sat cross-legged on the bank, and ordered the Indian to sleep, while he kept watch.

"Yes," said the Cree good-humoredly, "for we must keep our one foot strong, or else we cannot even hop along!"

"Tell me, Awaskees," asked the boy suddenly, "why you were willing to come on this trip, and what will become of your wife?"

"Why should a wife," said the Cree, "stand between a man and his fate?"

"But suppose she goes hungry?"

"It is not winter," answered Awaskees. "Like me, she has two hands to hold a fish spear. Like me she has two hands to hold a rifle. I have a child. It is her child also. I did not marry a flabby thing, such as that which the white man is sure to love, that would starve unless the acorns were husked for her, and the shells of the nuts cracked, and the berries picked from the bushes. My wife is a woman, Jimmy. Besides," he added, taking his last pull on his pipe, "if I live, he will make me rich."

And he pointed toward the sleeping form of Alabama Joe.

CHAPTER THIRTY-FIVE

BY THE EDGE of the stream sat Jimmy. He had in his well hand the base of a narrow pole which rested at the balance over one knee and extended out over the water, into which there dropped from the end of it a line that seemed to break off at a sharp angle as it reached the surface. There was not much chance of a fish, the boy felt, but it would be foolish to waste the hours of his watch. His bare feet, tough in the sole as moccasins, rested on the icy rocks which framed the shore. And a cold air bathed him, the damp, chill morning air of the woods.

Their camping place was on the margin of a bend, so that he could look both up and down the stream to a considerable distance, and in case another craft came in sight, he would be able to mark it well before it came close enough to see him through the showering branches which concealed his place on the bank. The canoe was high and dry, and covered over with branches. Not even a beaver, swimming down that stream, would have been able to distinguish the camouflage from real brush. So well did Awaskees understand his art!

Jimmy had seen this work before, and had admired it; but never before had he been with a man whose life, perhaps, depended upon good hiding, and he took careful note of everything. He felt, indeed, that he was living upon a different plane, and that six months of such life would teach him the woods as he never had known them before.

Every ten seconds, he looked up and down at the neighboring bends. They remained blank, though sometimes the force of the current, changing course a little, would appear to him like the shadow of an approaching boat, and he grew tense to observe it. Nothing came, as yet, and sleepiness was far from his eyes.

He began to think over all that had chanced to him. He began to turn the Southerner in his mind—or was he a Southerner indeed? He felt, in a way, that Alabama Joe was a force like a great wind, picking up and displacing other human lives like dead leaves, whirling them lightly before him, drifting them in heaps into new positions. He had come to Fort Anxious, and in so short a time he had transformed the business of the grocer; he had won the love of Carson's daughter; he had crushed the great reputation of the most important man in the Fort. He had beaten and disgraced the formidable brothers, those man-slaying Lafittes. And, besides this, he had opened the eyes of old Tyndal, and he had drawn upon his trail the vengeance of the law in the strong person of Charlie Dyce, and in the hatred of Parker.

Then the boy wondered profoundly whether he could call this criminal actually a bad man, or a good one. He could not tell. There had been moments when he himself had been in mortal fear of the hands of the Stingaree. At other moments, he felt himself close as a blood brother to the man. No, he could not make a moral pronouncement and say good or bad about a thing which appeared to be, above all, a sheer force.

By the strong light which the Stingaree cast upon all those who were near him, the Cree was newly seen, likewise. He had always seemed to Jimmy about perfect, but now there were other things to say about Awaskees. He had proved himself braver and more ready of wit than ever. But he also had established himself as a distinctly practical mind. He came on this trip, he had said, out of love for Jimmy Green; and yet out of his own lips he was convicted of having the highest hopes of practical benefits to be showered upon him at a later date by the criminal, as a reward for deliverance. Was that noble? No, it was not.

Yet it was forgivable, Jimmy felt. For the Indian had sensed in the tramp a power which would be able to endow friends richly. Highly forgivable, then, was the attitude of Awaskees, the moose hunter.

What of Charlie Dyce—youthful hero of Fort Anxious, about whom every one spoke a good word?

No, not altogether perfect was even Charlie Dyce, for he worked partly for the fun of the game, and partly for a better salary; and partly for fame, which in reality was a god with clay feet.

As for Jimmy himself?

He looked deeply inward, and sighed.

Truly he wished to serve and save the big man from the South. But also he had come because of the relish of the adventure; and the joy of pitting himself with one party of strong men against another party, almost equally keen, far greater in numbers. In a sense, he wanted to be a brave and faithful friend. And in another sense, he wanted to "show off" before the eyes of the mysterious Stingaree.

More mysterious, to be sure, the more Jimmy knew about him.

So Jimmy, sighing over these problems, reached a conclusion which older and wiser philosophers had reached before him—that there is nothing human that is also pure. Only in heaven can absolute love, faith, and service be found.

Something stirred. He looked behind him and saw the great head and the eyes of Mishe Mukwa, always green with suspicion.

He, too, was a problem, for he had come to the service of

Alabama Joe partly from love, but partly from fear; and fear, surely, had in the first place controlled him.

Indeed, the longer Jimmy thought over these problems, the more convinced he became that only one thing was worth his attention, and that was the power of Alabama Joe.

In what that power consisted he could not pretend to say. It was, doubtless, made of many parts. This was a juggler, a safe-cracker, a most eminent liar, a thief, a house-breaker, a highway robber, a smooth-spoken deceiver, a male flirt and gunman. But he was something beyond all this. All these things added together did not quite explain the attraction which drew men, and women, and animals to him.

Something flashed at the upper bend.

Jimmy, seeing it, beached his fishing rod instantly, and then saw a canoe with four paddlers. It drew nearer. He could swear that there was no pair of shoulders in it equal to those of big Stanley Parker, and nowhere did he see a silhouette similar to the familiar contour of Charlie Dyce.

No, it turned out to be a ragged set of voyageurs, with a heap of packs in the center of a big canoe as delicate, as decorated, as exquisite as the paddlers were beggarly.

They went by, and turning the bend, all at once they struck up a paddling song, and the strange, broken rhythm wavered through the air, and enchanted the forest, and the ear of Jimmy Green.

They disappeared around the bend, and he found himself nodding and smiling.

They were not enemies! Enemies to nothing except themselves, when whisky was cheap. He sighed and smiled again. Not enemies? he repeated in his thought. Enemies, of course. For all men were hostile, since if they were not actually upon the trail of the fugitives, they could give warning to others who were, and every craft that floated upon those waters was a potential cruiser coming against them. All the arms of the law could make them. All the money of the law could hire paddlers and riflemen.

It was a new thought, and Jimmy winced as it came into his mind.

Slowly he pushed the fishing rod out again, and the bait dropped with a careless flop into the water.

Well, no matter for that, since nothing was biting in these shallows and could not be expected to bite. The bait was dead, moreover, and Jimmy knew that he was going through

144

a mere form of fishing. He had barely reached this conclusion when the rod was almost snatched from his hands!

He managed to keep some sort of grip with one hand, being jerked to his feet with the rush of the weight on the other end of the line.

But then he had both hands on it and braced himself as the fish changed and bolted up the stream.

He drew in what play he could of the rod, to meet the shock as the big fellow came to the end of its run.

The fish was turning. And Jimmy, filled with a sudden inspiration, ran inshore and jerked hard. Luck was with him. The fish jumped. Its head was so big that the sight of the great lake trout frightened him, but that leap threw it off balance, and the next moment it was wriggling on the bank.

And yet Jimmy had little joy of his prize. He knew it was not landed or hooked by his skill. A ghostly feeling came to him that the evil spirits or good who watched over Alabama Joe had sent this prize to their servant!

CHAPTER THIRTY-SIX

IT IS MORE than odd that this famous hunt of the Indian, the boy, and the criminal should be called by none of their names. Even Mishe Mukwa might well have been honored. Or failing that, the trail might have been ascribed to Charlie Dyce, whose work was such an honor, even to the Northwest Mounted. However, the affair is now known from the Pacific to the Atlantic as the "Parker Trail." No one can tell why, unless because a magazine article told of the first events of the man hunt before it was even completed. The writer called the chase "The Parker Trail," and by this name it is now known everywhere.

Every detail of it cannot be told, but a few of the most important and striking facts must be catalogued.

For instance: They made a five-hour halt at that first stopping place, when the Indian rose without a yawn and without a word, and sat down to eat a great slab of the fish which the boy had roasted over a small, smokeless fire. Between them, they barely managed to rouse Alabama Joe, but once the smell of food reached him, he seemed quite recovered. He sat down cross-legged, and the three of them feasted. There was enough for them all, and finally to satisfy the huge hunger of Mishe.

Having eaten and covered the trace of the fire, they put out into the stream, and paddled easily down the current.

Not a word was spoken. Alabama Joe, taking his place in the middle of the craft with his head on an edge of the pack in lieu of a pillow, instantly fell asleep again, with his poulticed hands laid across his breast. Jimmy took his place in the bow, for his own wound had recovered wonderfully. Holding the paddle in his sound right hand, he could push on the very tip of the hilt with the heel of the injured member, and so he managed to give real help to Awaskees.

It was not vigorous paddling, but it was enough to keep them spinning along at a good gait, with the current helping mightily. That same current, unluckily, was helping their pursuers, and Jimmy was not surprised when, about noon in the day, he heard a low word from the Indian, and looked back to find that a four-paddle canoe was coming swiftly after them.

Charlie Dyce had taken his men to an outlying trapper's hut, where they were able to buy a boat, and in this—a dugout, but a trimly made one—they had set off down the stream. The strokes of four paddles were more than twice as effective as the work of a man and a half, which was about the useful strength of Awaskees and his crippled crew. So, at noon in the day, Jimmy looked back and saw them coming.

Speed would not help them now. Instinctively he looked toward the shore, though Alabama Joe might prove even more of a helpless leviathan in the woods than he had been so far on the river. But, since they had to take to the land, it seemed far better to do so at once and gain as much of a lead as possible before allowing their pursuers to close up the gap between the two canoes.

Yet, though he looked back repeatedly, there was no sign from Awaskees, who kept on paddling.

They rounded a long curve, and as the trees shut out the view of the rearward boat, a new thought came to Jimmy, and instantly he had dropped his paddle and was stripping off his clothes. A mere wriggle was sufficient to shed most of them, once a fastening or two had been loosed.

Then, in spite of his haste, he could not help trying the water with his hand, boy fashion, and shuddering as the ice of it ran up into his blood. That hesitation was only for an instant, and then he stood up and leaped from the center of the canoe into the air so expertly that the light craft only staggered a little from the thrust of his feet.

So Jimmy Green flashed through the sunlight in a bright arc, and disappeared into the face of the river with not much more noise than a fish of the same size would have made in slipping home. A tuft of leaves was floating down the current. As he rose, he caught this small branch; and giving one glance toward the rapidly retreating back of Awaskees, he covered his face with the leaves and lay close to the surface, swimming just hard enough to keep his head pointed upstream.

He was naked. But he had brought with him the tool which he wanted, and that was his long-bladed hunting knife, with an edge of which even Awaskees had approved.

He carried it in his teeth, gripped by the blade, and the taste of the steel was like the taste of this adventure, as he saw the canoe of Dyce come spinning around the curve.

There was in it as formidable an array of faces as one could have picked out of the populace of Fort Anxious. For he saw there Dyce in the bow; and big Stanley Parker's weight stowed at the stern, where the greatest burden should be. And in between these two appeared Louis Dupres, a half-breed with the cunning of an Indian and the rash valor of a white desperado; and behind Dupres appeared the broad, brutal face of Butch Graham, whose savagery was so intense that he would chase the youngsters. He had caught eight-year-old Sammy Webster and thrown him off the edge of the bluff below the Sampson house. The depth of the pool of water at its base kept Sammy's neck intact, and prevented Butch from being lynched. Jimmy Green, as he stared out through the leaves, wondered again and again that Charlie Dyce had selected such traveling mates.

Certainly, sterling goodness had not been what he was after! But, after all, the end was the thing for him, and not the means toward it. He could not have found in the Northwest three more powerful canoe men, or much better woodsmen, either. These fellows all would march until they starved on their feet; Butch and Louis because they had the instincts of hunting dogs, and Stanley Parker because he was controlled and consumed by hunger for revenge. It seemed to the boy that he could read this emotion in the face of Parker, even at a distance; and he grew colder than even the temperature of the water. Charlie Dyce, he knew, was the fairest man in the world; but Jimmy would rather have trusted his life to a puma than to any of the other three!

As he measured the distance and watched the canoe come closer, with a wonderful unison and rhythm of paddle strokes, Jimmy could not help admiring this beautiful machine. He admired it, and then dived.

He thought at first that he had waited too long, and that the canoe had passed on above him, hurled along by the current, and by the four pairs of arms; but when he looked up through the water toward the blue dazzle of the sky, suddenly the nose of the canoe appeared, with its bow wave curling and flashing like liquid diamond. Toward the belly of the shadow Jimmy rose, striking out with his hands until he was very close. He feared, even now, that it might escape from him, but he was over-anxious.

He reached it a third of the way from the stern, and ripping across and downward, he opened a great, ragged hole through which he could guess how the water was bursting upward. He stabbed again. The point of the knife struck wood, but he wrenched it out and had time for a third blow, which laid open the end of the canoe and let the flood in there also.

He rose to the surface.

"Rocks, rocks!" he heard Butch Graham yelling in his thick, horrible voice. "You dang chump, Parker, you! Rocks you put us on—"

Jimmy took a deep breath and dived again, triumphant, for he had seen the canoe rapidly sinking.

The stream whirled him along with a strong hand; and as he rose to the surface again, safely in the distance, he saw the four struggling with bending paddles toward the nearest shore, but with the water gunwale high.

It now went in over the lip of the canoe's side. In another moment, he heard the enormous voice of Butch thundering curses.

The canoe was down!

He had hoped that it would sink in such deep water that it could not be reclaimed. As it was, the voyage of the four must be delayed for hours while they repaired the damage which he had done, and Jimmy Green swam on, laughing with pleasure.

Then, as he came to the bend, he heard a loud shouting. A rifle clanged. A bullet cut the surface an inch from his nose and doused his face with stinging spray.

When he looked back, he saw that madman, Butch Graham, struggling to get his rifle free for a second shot, while Charlie Dyce, of course, was preventing him.

Then the current snaked Jimmy around an arm of projecting rocks, and he was out of view.

There was no canoe before him.

He took to the shore and ran down it, going hard to get his blood warm again, and as he ran, lightly, strongly, it seemed to Jimmy that the world was a better place than ever it had been before.

For this was a marvel of which Fort Anxious well could talk.

Yes, and it did so, telling how one boy met four strong men, all armed to the teeth, and stopped them, and sank their boat, and caused them the loss of a good bit of the best powder, and of two excellent repeating rifles which, together with all the weapons, had gone to the bottom of the stream. The rest were reclaimed, but now the party had two long-distance weapons alone.

Jimmy could not know this, but he had done enough to delight himself even without that knowledge; and when he came in view of the canoe, he whooped like a young hunting wolf.

So much so, indeed, that Mishe Mukwa stood up and smiled to show all his teeth.

The Indian, however, pointed ahead to a spot where some shelving rocks ran out into good deep water. There the boy ran, and there Awaskees paused to let him spring aboard.

He went again into the bow and there he kneeled, swinging the paddle rhythmically, his heart light, his very soul uplifted in the expectation of praise.

Not a word of it came to him. Not a syllable of commendation did they speak, and yet he bitterly told himself that they would already be in the hands of the law, if it had not been for his exploit.

All day they went on, with the tramp sleeping like one possessed in the bottom of the canoe. All day they slid on northward, and when dusk came, they paused again for a brief meal of fish, which had been caught by trolling on the way. But before they stopped, Awaskees said:

"Brother!"

"Aye!" said Jimmy shortly.

"Is it time to rest and eat?"

Jimmy could not speak. He could only nod. For he saw that though no praise had come to him, by this feat today he had made himself a man, and equal to either of the others. Even Awaskees would condescend to ask his advice.

CHAPTER THIRTY-SEVEN

THE PLAN of their march was now laid on a large scale. The three had started north, and now in solemn council they voted on the way they should continue—to turn back south, once more, or to strike on northward, either aiming at Hudson Bay or Alaska; or else to swing west, cross the great divide into British Columbia, and then follow the rivers down to the sea. In the course of such a journey they should have a fair chance of shaking off all pursuit, and coming out of the woods their own masters, with even Charlie Dyce baffled behind them. The longest way round was taken to be the safest. It could be taken for granted that all the ways south would be most carefully watched, from this time forward; and that while they were watched, it would be a vastly difficult thing to break across the border.

So all three, one by one, voted for the northern march, to be followed by a crossing of the great mountains, and then the descent to the Pacific. It might take weeks, it might take months to accomplish this trek. No one could tell, really, how long it would be. Currents, portages, a thousand things had to be considered.

And they worked north up the lonely rivers. Wounded hands were healed. Incessant labor made them hard as leather, and their muscles turned to rubbery strings, incapable of fatigue. Meat was their diet, and they did not have to hunt for it on shore, for the silent sliding canoe gave them many a glimpse of deer lifting their dripping muzzles from the water's edge, and whirling too late to escape from the rifle bullet.

They had plenty of chances, now, to observe the skill of Alabama Joe with a rifle. It mattered not what part of a split second remained to him to make his shot, he could snatch up a weapon from the bottom of the canoe and with a bullet that seemed unaimed, he never once failed to strike the target. He shot squirrels out of high branches with no more seeming difficulty than he planted slugs behind the shoulders of deer.

Such shooting Jimmy had heard talked of, but he never had seen before, and he and Awaskees exchanged many a glance. Compliments, however, there were none. As on the day of his famous swim and his attack on the canoe of Charlie Dyce and his three desperate companions, so now; no matter what happened, there was no interchange of compliments. They kept their breath, as it were, for the necessary labor of paddling. When the light and the water permitted, they kept going twenty-four hours of the day, resting and paddling in relays. And when they went ashore, they strove to fire-dry more meat than they could eat, so that there would be provisions on hand in the next pinch.

Meat without salt, roasted in gobbets on the end of wooden splinters and, therefore, sometimes half raw, sometimes half turned to cinders, was the main fuel which they burned in their three furnaces, supplying power.

Such power, too!

Their shoulders bulged with strength. They were machines. And constant practice had taught the Stingaree enough of the art so that, with his enormous strength, he was able to drive the canoe along even more swiftly than Awaskees.

They passed on that voyage an occasional canoe, which did not stop them, when seeing the insistent paddling of Awaskees and his men. They passed, once, a big raft, loaded high, and two men guarding the load with aggressive rifles. But on the whole they saw few people, and day after day they were alone.

It would have been a very silent trip, except that Alabama Joe was always willing to talk and tell stories, not of his own experiences, but of those of certain carelessly named people to whom he would refer, as:

"There was a fellow in Chicago by name of Slim Jerry"— or, "Once I was riding a Colorado trail like Ike the Dustman."

These stories were so fascinating to Jimmy that he could have listened to them forever, but forever he did not have. Only a snatch here and there as they were cooking on shore, or perhaps a fragment when, by mutual consent, they stopped paddling hard and enjoyed the power of the current.

So they went north. They became a machine. If a deer, a bear, or any other game were killed, each knew his share, whether it were picking feathers, skinning, quartering, cutting meat in strips and chunks, gathering wood, building fires, keeping watch. Not a word was necessary to the progress of the business.

Mishe Mukwa, during this time, gradually had been adjusting himself to the crew. He accepted Jimmy as one whom he had already known; it took longer for him to allow Awaskees to come near without baring his teeth; but he controlled himself eventually, though he never showed the slightest affection for any one but his chosen master. Crouched before him in the canoe, or stretched at his feet on shore, the great dog never left him.

And neither Jimmy nor Awaskees ever complained about the extra burden which the big dog made in the boat or mentioned the uselessness of such a weight. They knew that the Stingaree would not dream for an instant of continuing his journey without the brute.

They reached Lake Charming and found ducks and black divers on its waters. And in the evening they heard the booming call of the loon. That night they went ashore and luxuriated on roast duck. They pushed off in the morning in a strong east wind, which they utilized by erecting a small, strong sail, and this drove them steadily up a western tributary of the lake for two whole days, until the wind failed and the current grew stronger. After that, began a new form of labor.

They ran two lines to the canoe and warped it up the shore, in the still water. On one line, Mishe Mukwa pulled with the might of a strong man—Awaskees had fashioned for him a neat leather harness. On the other line pulled one of the three; a second went beside the canoe to guide it with a pole around obstructions, and a third went ahead to scout the easiest way. They pushed on for a week, in this manner, then rested a day, and again continued. The western mountains began to grow up before them. For a fortnight they had not seen a human being.

There was no thought of failure, now. It seemed that the trail they traveled had been too complicated and twisting to be followed even by a Charlie Dyce; and the only thought that they kept before them was of the long leagues of labor which lay ahead.

They reached the foothills. The mountains rose close before them in the day and marched back into the blue distance in morning and evening.

On such a morning they had barely rigged their lines and started the journey for the day, when around the lower curve of the stream they saw a similar party approaching them—two men on tow lines, another beside the canoe with a pole, and a fourth in advance to pick the way. One glance was enough. The bulky shoulders of Stanley Parker would have been distinguishable at thrice that distance!

All heart left them, for the moment. The victorious cheer of the trailers, coming dim and faint through the thin, upland air, stunned the three fugitives, for it seemed that the trailers had accomplished a feat more than human in clinging to the way so long! By what clues had they proceeded? What chance information had they picked up here and there from voyageurs? Or upon the merest hints had they fathomed the minds of the trio and struck up this river by chance? What huge patience, therefore, had theirs been in trudging on day after day, accepting the most bitter labor, until, at last, they came upon the sign of the three men and the dog. Aye, by the trail of the dog they could have guessed the truth!

Luckily, the way of the stream was very crooked and angling. Awaskees pulled with the force of more than a man, now; or, at least, with a far greater endurance. They made good time, and, struggle as they might, the party of four could not gain.

Only twice did they try rifle shots at the crew of the Stingaree. Those bullets went wide. The distance increased. And then only three men were seen at the canoe. The fourth had disappeared, no doubt to try to gain on an overland march, and come up to pick off at least one of the fugitives.

Evening came down on that bitter day. They were too tired to speak. They could only constantly lean on the lines, and turn their heads now and again to search the brush for ambush. But who could really probe some of those thickets? The light had grown so dim that marksmanship seemed out of the question, when they reached a bare point around which the current slid with a loud, rushing sound. Opposite them were larch and tall firs. At the neck of the little headland appeared a shadowy clustering of brush, faintly starred with flowers even in this dull light. Never would Jimmy forget that place. For as they reached it, a rifle rang with terrible loudness from the bushes, and Awaskees stumbled, and let the pull line sag a bit over his shoulder.

He was hurt. How badly, it would have been hard to say, since he instantly resumed his pull.

But the Stingaree went for the brush like a wild beast. He went running low, dodging behind bushes, behind rocks, and darting in with a wonderful swiftness. He had left his rifle behind. A revolver was in his hand, and death, Jimmy knew, was in his thoughts.

He disappeared in the brush. Then two quick shots followed. They could hear a dashing of a runner through the shrubbery. Silence followed.

Rounding the point, Awaskees paused to open his trouser leg and show a deep flesh wound through his outer thigh. He washed and bandaged it, and marched on; while Jimmy, with a sense of utter ruin, stared at him and felt they were defeated. He could march now. He never would be able to do so when the wound grew cold and the torn muscles began to ache.

And the Stingaree?

He was gone. He did not reappear. One of those two rifle bullets, no doubt, had reached his body, and the pursuers were now in no haste, having reached the prize they wanted.

Mishe Mukwa, in a frenzy as he saw his master disappear, had severed the line with one slash of his teeth and gone after him into the brush. He also, refused to return, and before the mind of Jimmy grew up a horrible picture of the dead man on his back, and the great beast crouched beside him, on guard!

Still they pulled patiently forward, helpless and hopeless, but unwilling to surrender. Utter darkness came before Awaskees raised his hand and signaled that this was the right place. Right, Jimmy guessed, because more steps had become impossible to the limping Indian.

CHAPTER THIRTY-EIGHT

MOURNFUL WAS that camp. Awaskees, in a murmur, pointed out the herbs which he wished the boy to gather. When they were brought, the Indian chewed them, and made a poultice over the wound. Then he ate some sun-jerked venison, and putting his back against a tree, he deliberately loaded and lighted a pipe; as though he scorned precautions, now, and bade his enemies come take him.

Were those patient hunters now scouting ahead along the river to find the crippled Indian and his party?

"Awaskees," broke out the boy at last, intolerably impatient, "tell me if the Stingaree is gone!"

The Indian inhaled a long puff and blew the smoke slowly upward, a barely distinguishable mist in the darkness.

"He is coming now," he said at last, "to tell you what he has done."

Jimmy gaped. But when he put his ear to the ground, he thought he heard noises like the approach of one not too light of foot in the forest. Then a big shadow detached itself from the brush. It was the big man himself!

He would not speak, at first. He got a long strip of venison and chewed it up without saying a word. Then he followed the example of Awaskees and lighted a smoke.

At last he said: "How is your leg, Awaskees?"

"I shall not walk in the morning," said the Cree cheerfully. "I can crawl, but not fast enough to go with you, brother."

To this the other did not reply, but after a time he muttered: "I missed him. It was dark. He dodged like a flying duck. He got away."

He made another pause and then said: "I went down the river and found them. I came up to them—as close as this. I'm no woodsman, either, but that was like burglary."

He laughed a little, hardly louder than a whisper. And the teeth of the boy were set on edge.

Mishe Mukwa came out of the dark and lay panting at the feet of the master. Something had made him pause behind.

"There was no light, but I could have got me a pair of

them, at least," said the Stingaree. "Maybe a third. They were talking louder than the river noise. They were laughing —except Dyce. He's a man. The others are wolves. I would have slaughtered 'em. But there's the law. Or maybe I've lost my nerve. I couldn't shoot!"

No one made comment. And Jimmy heard the gritting of the teeth of Alabama Joe, ground hard together.

"Now you have rested long enough," said Awaskees. "It is time for you to march. Leave the canoe. You cannot pull that up the stream. They would surely overtake you. It would be more than an Indian that they would shoot down the next time!"

It was the only bitterness that Jimmy ever had heard in the speech of the red man, and he went on:

"Make a good march before morning. Mishe Mukwa will carry part of the pack."

"We stay with you," said Alabama Joe bluntly.

"There is no good—" began Awaskees.

"We stay with you!" said the Stingaree, his voice loud and fierce.

A faint echo came out from among the trees. To Jimmy it seemed to say: "Dead, dead!"

Before the sun set again, there would be an end to them all. He looked up. There were many clouds in the sky. Besides, the trees closed over their heads, but through a small gap in the branches, he could see the bright glimmer of one star. And it seemed to Jimmy that the character of the Stingaree was like that overcast heaven, with one bright star in it.

"The kid, though," said the Stingaree. "Here, lad, make your pack! Take that light rifle. You slide out. You're no good to us now. Get out, and get fast!"

Jimmy sighed a little. He hardly heard the words—so keenly had he been expecting them that it seemed to him he had heard them before.

"I stay with you," he said without interest.

"You danged little fool!" exclaimed the Stingaree. "D'you simply want to be another burden on our hands?"

But it was too patent, and Jimmy looked easily through the words. He could see all that was coming—the camp made here—the attack through the woods—the cracking of the guns—the whistling of the bullets, and death coming to them, one by one. He saw the picture, but it had no serious meaning to him, for Alabama Joe had pointed out the path of duty.

So Jimmy laughed a little softly.

"I stay with you," he repeated.

"You mean—" began Joe.

Then Awaskees broke in gently: "See, brother. He also is a man."

After that, there was no more persuasion, and Awaskees added suddenly: "I can sit up and keep a watch, however. You two sleep. I shall sit and watch."

They were half blind with fatigue. They dropped off asleep instantly, and the last that Jimmy saw was the very faint profile of the Indian, half lost in the night.

He wakened later, with the barking of guns far down the river. The Stingaree already was on his feet.

The noise of guns stopped.

"He's given us the slip," said he.

"Who, Joe?"

"Awaskees. He knew that the canoe was no more good to us. He's taken it and gone down the river. Taken a rifle and a paddle, and that's all. With a game leg to drag around. One chance in five of living through it, but he wouldn't be a weight on us! He's gone!"

"He's gone!" gasped Jimmy.

It seemed impossible. They had been together so long, the three of them, that it was like waking to find a member of the body gone.

"Pack!" said the Stingaree sternly. "And we march."

They packed and started. In an hour, the dawn began, but still they trudged on. Only once the Stingaree paused and said gloomily:

"Did they get him as he drifted by their camp? If they did, I'll have their blood for it. I'll have the four of them!"

They marched all day, making only brief halts. They climbed high. The mountains went up before them like a wall, split by the single pass for which they headed. Climbing along a narrow ridge, they looked far down to the left and saw there in a valley a little village.

Jimmy looked at it as at another world. There were black and green patches of fallow and of crop land. The sunlight trembled and flashed on windows. The smoke went crookedly upward. And all they had done seemed foolish and

157

dreamlike—to see now fixed human habitations, and fixed human lives, rooted like trees in one soil.

Night came. It was bitterly cold after sun fall. A wind dropped from the upper snows. They were high up. Each breath reached the bottom of the lungs, and the cold burned them. They lay in a close huddle, the dog and the two men. Still they shuddered.

The moon rose. Between its light and the freezing, they were constantly rousing. Once Jimmy wakened and found that his arms were clasped tightly around the neck of Mishe, pulling the great formidable head closer to his body. The dog was panting, but he had not stirred in protest.

It was not more than midnight when the hand of the man touched Jimmy's shoulder, and the boy sat up with a start.

"Listen!" said the Stingaree.

The boy listened, and he heard far off beneath them the sound of dogs baying in a deep-throated chorus.

"They got dogs on us!" said Jimmy. "Oh, dang 'em! They got dogs onto our trail, Joe!"

The latter already was making up the pack. And they went on through the iron jaws of the pass, which rang and echoed like the metal itself under the noise of the wind. They had to lean against that cruel, biting force. Once or twice, as the way narrowed, and the wind increased, Jimmy found himself blown to a standstill, leaning forward at an angle of forty-five degrees.

The moon, too, was as cruel as the wind; it seemed to give eyes and wicked intelligence to the tooth of the cold, telling it where to strike.

And as they clambered high on the trail, getting toward the snow line, suddenly the big arm of the tramp went around the shoulders of the boy. He pointed down to what looked like the reflection of a star.

"That's a house down there, Jimmy. Warm blankets, hot coffee, steaks and eggs, likely. Go on down there. You don't belong here. This is my business, and not yours!"

But Jimmy laughed.

"I'll stay, Joe," said he.

The latter did not try to dissuade him again.

They marched. The trees dwindled. The terrible wind totally unmasked, froze them to the bone; and behind them, the dogs clamored more loudly.

"Bloodhounds—otherwise they wouldn't be stickin' to the trail so close," commented Jimmy.

The big man said nothing at all, until Jimmy cried out suddenly. "Mishe Mukwa! Where is he?"

The Stingaree turned around.

"He'd stand anything but the cold, maybe," he said after a moment. "He's gone for warmed diggings, Jimmy. Well—he was a good dog while he lasted!"

"Look!" cried Jimmy. "There he goes, now!"

The big outline of the wolf dog appeared where the trail narrowed and sharply turned a shoulder of the cliff behind them. They looked across a deep, narrow valley. Mishe Mukwa had traveled back half a mile to reach this point!

Having reached it, he did not go on. There he paused, crouched in the moonlight, plainly visible.

The song of the hounds roared loudly across the valley.

And now they came in view, their noses close to the trail—five monsters, able to pull down deer, or men.

"Look!" said the Stingaree. "He's not running away. He's gone to be our rear guard!"

CHAPTER THIRTY-NINE

THE FORCE of the wind and the cold were forgotten by Jimmy Green as he stared back across the deep shadows of the canyon to where the wolf dog stood in the keen light of the moon, for he wondered if his companion could possibly be right.

However, the question was quickly solved.

The first hound, with lumbering stride, rounded the shoulder of the hill well in advance of its fellows, and Mishe Mukwa was upon it before it could so much as throw up its head. Jimmy saw the snap of a fighting wolf, which knows how to throw its weight into the slash of its fangs. He saw the shoulder of Mishe smite the side of the other, and the big dog shot from the trail into empty air.

It turned over, sprawling, before the first note of its death cry reached Jimmy's ear, and dropped out of sight into the shadows of the canyon.

The next two came almost abreast. The outer one, Mishe

served exactly as he had the first of these trailers. There was one snap, one shoulder thrust, and the poor dog fell down through empty space, headfirst, howling. The second already had its grip on the flank of the wolf dog; but a moment later it lay on its back, twisting, writhing, helpless, while Mishe arose to face the charge of the last pair.

They held back a little from this incarnate death. They looked over their shoulders toward the men who labored up the trail well behind; but Mishe did not pause. He charged straight home and involved himself in a spinning tangle.

Jimmy held his breath. He reached out his hand, and found it gripped hard, that instant, by Alabama Joe.

"You didn't send him, Joe?" he gasped.

"How could I send him?" growled the tramp. "He went—that's all!"

They saw the men running up from behind.

Then one dog rose from the tangle and sprang back—Mishe Mukwa, with two more enemies left on the trail squirming, and one of them kicking in such a blind agony that it tipped itself over the edge of the cliff.

"Run, Mishe, run!" screamed Jimmy Green, dancing with impatience.

But Mishe either was too badly hurt to run, or else his blood was up and he disdained flight. Planting his feet, he waited for the men themselves; and Jimmy saw the leader—a tall man with great spreading shoulders, who looked like Parker, certainly—pitch a gun butt to his shoulder. Mishe fell prostrate in the trail. The noise of the gun boomed hollow across the gorge, and Jimmy turned, half sick, in time to see that his companion had raised his own rifle to avenge that fall. He gripped the barrel of the gun and dragged it down.

"Don't shoot, Joe," he gasped.

"Dang him! I'll have his life!" said Alabama Joe fiercely, and knocked the boy away.

Back staggered Jimmy. He felt the thinness of the air behind him. He struggled to get his balance. Yes, and would have gained it again, just as Joe reached for him with a horrified face. But a strong gust of wind caught at him—struck him with a heavy hand—and he dropped into space.

The dreadful moment endured long enough to let him have one thought—that he was the third to go for the Stingaree. Then he struck heavily on a rock ledge, not six feet below the upper rim of the trail.

He stood up, gasping, laughing weakly. The instant his weight came onto his right foot, the ankle gave with a grinding pain, and he knew that it was either broken or terribly sprained. But the great hand of Alabama Joe reached for him and lifted him strongly up. It was like being heaved by a powerful machine that landed him breathless in the trail again.

There he sank to one knee.

"Kid," said the Stingaree, "are you hurt?"

There was something desperate and quiet in that voice which made Jimmy look up to him in amazement.

"I'm all right," said he, "but I can't go on. I've given my ankle a twist. That's all. Sorry, old-timer. Go on and beat 'em. They'll never catch you. Look! Yonder's the divide, I reckon. Get on over it, Joe. You'll have a down slope, then. You're as good as back in Alabama now. I wish I was, too!"

He laughed again, but it was not a very strong laugh, for as the blood came to the hurt ankle, he was giddy with pain.

He was raised in the strong arms of Joe.

"Leave me be, Joe," said he. "I'm gunna rustle for myself, pretty good! They'll run you down!"

"They've turned back, Jimmy," said Alabama Joe. "Otherwise, I might even leave you in the trail for them to pick up. Charlie Dyce is a white man. He wouldn't harm you, son. But they've turned back, and I'll find a camping ground for us, tonight."

"You're white," said Jimmy. "You're dang white, Joe!"

With cold and labor he was weak. Perhaps that was why the wave of pain seemed to run from his foot all through his body and burst in darkness upon his brain. At any rate, he sagged helplessly in the strong arms of the Stingaree, and the latter went on with great strides, calling to the boy, as though he were at a distance and simply had to be overtaken.

Then he stopped to tear off his coat and wrap the cold body in this.

But that was vain. The wind was edged. It penetrated the blood and bone of Jimmy Green, and roused him from his fainting spell to a shuddering life.

"Leave me be, Stingaree," he gasped. "I'm gunna come through all right. I don't need no help—I can manage fine—"

"Sure you can," said the Stingaree cheerfully, "but you wouldn't want to have me camp out up here all alone, Jim, would you?"

He turned from the trail and climbed into a scattering of lodge-pole pines. He began to crunch through snow. Then he dipped into a hollow where the force of the wind dropped away to nothing, and the trees were thick.

There he paused.

Holding Jimmy in the hollow of one arm with wonderful strength, he slashed off enough boughs to make him a sitting place free from the snow.

His speed was extraordinary as he put Jimmy down and went on gathering wood.

And the boy sat up and set his teeth against the burning, throbbing pain which swelled his leg. He smiled against the exquisite torment, and said:

"You seen them turn back, Joe?"

"Yeah."

"Their hearts are broke! They've had enough. They've tried you on water, and they tried you on dry land, and they've tried you with dogs, and you've beat them every time. They'll never try to foller you through the snows, Joe. You're as good as home, and ain't I glad!"

To his own deliverance, the Stingaree paid no attention. He merely said:

"How are you now, son?"

"Me? Aw, fine," said Jimmy. "Never b-b-b-etter."

He could not keep his teeth from clattering in the cold. His lips, too, were thick with it.

In the meantime, the strokes of the little hand-ax had swished off boughs and lopped saplings, slicing through four-inch trunks at a single blow. A wind shelter was reared in the fashion which Awaskees taught—the best of all fashions in the wilderness. And then a fire was lighted and the tea kettle filled with snow to melt and boil. A bed was next built close under the shelter. And Jimmy Green crawled onto it and laid himself down, the blood spinning in his brain.

The first hot water was for the dressing and bathing of the ankle. It was already swollen incredibly big, and the feel of the hot water was like a touch from heaven to suffering Jimmy. Then Stingaree bound the ankle tight. The grip of those bandages was a pain, at first, but then, like the pressure of a firm but kindly hand, it shut the torment away.

Jimmy put his back against a nearby tree.

He was out of his immediate trouble, in one way, but in another he still felt very odd. It was unlike anything that he ever had known in all his days. The snow, the trees, the fire, and the face of Alabama Joe seemed to lift and waver like flames. He shut his eyes, but the odd up-and-down continued in his own mind. He wedged his back against a tree and made himself smile at the fire. Then the Stingaree put a piece of jerked venison into his hands and Jimmy found, to his utter amazement, that he had no appetite. No, the venison was actually revolting to him.

He pretended to eat, the while looking on at the hearty appetite of his friend with bewilderment. A keen pain, also, began to clamor in his breast, stabbing deep and a little deeper with every breath that he drew.

"You look a little white, Jim," said Alabama Joe.

"Me. I'm fine," said Jimmy. "I've had enough to eat, though. I'm gunna sleep."

"That'll fix you better than anything, Jim."

"Joe, I'd sleep better if you'd tell me that in the morning you'll hike along and leave me here. I could do fine. Somebody'll come along. Only get me back onto the trail—"

Alabama Joe raised his hand.

"Awaskees, and then Mishe," said he. "D'you think that I'll let you go, too, Jimmy? Never in the world!"

The boy did not argue.

For some reason, every word that he spoke was like money spent out of an almost empty purse. He could not understand this dreamy weakness.

The fire was split into two parts by the tramp. Between the sections was the bed. Warmth bathed Jimmy Green. Contentment began to sweep over him, and sleep rose like a great wave, filling his body, filling his soul. But though he closed his eyes, through the lashes he kept his attention fixed upon one great, staring star in the wind-scoured heavens, a star so bright that the moon could not put it out.

CHAPTER FORTY

HE HEARD THE DEEP, regular breathing of his companion presently. He wondered at it. It was the first time since the departure from Fort Anxious, a long time ago, that they had made camp and fallen asleep without leaving a watch. And he guessed by this that Alabama Joe was careless and desperate, or else that he was confident the enemy had definitely turned back from the trail. The latter hope was the true explanation, Jimmy thought.

And now the Stingaree would break through the mountains, find the ocean-going river, and down it float easily in some dugout or canoe of his finding or making. He was almost a woodsman, now, and he could not fail in the great task. It seemed to Jimmy like the victory of four over four million. It was the greatest thing that ever had happened in the world's history. With Awaskees and Mishe, he would be remembered for his share in that herculean march.

He sat up.

At once his head swayed back and forth, and all the mountains wavered before him like vast shadows.

"I'm kinda sick," said Jimmy to himself. "I guess I'm kinda bilious," he added.

The Widow Murphy always had declared that dizziness was a sign of an upset stomach.

He crawled with snaky softness to a large, white-faced stone that stood near one of the fires, and on this he wrote with a bit of charcoal:

Dear Joe: I wouldn't hang on and spoil things for you. I'll get along fine. You go and beat the game, and remember your partner,

Jim.

He finished writing this, and hesitated, wishing that he had the words to add more to it, for he realized that he was only expressing a small bit of what he felt. He wanted to put down something that would fully express his emotions. He knew that he had come to love the big man, and never so well as at this moment of parting from him. But no words occurred to Jimmy.

Something of his strength, also, was ebbing from him at every moment, and he decided that he had better get to a good distance as quickly as he could, so he dropped the charcoal and crawled away through the snow.

This was a disagreeable business. The snow which had felt so delightfully cool at first, now cut his hands with its sharp-edged crust; and he was continually breaking through, and having to wallow along forward like an amphibious creature, unsupplied with proper means of locomotion on the land.

But he managed, at last, to get up the side of the hollow, and after that the wind had him in its hands, as it were. It tumbled and rolled him. He gave his ankle a dozen twists and strains. And yet at the last, more than half frozen, he was out there on the open trail.

Then he found, to his amazement, that he could not tell which was the back trail and which was the forward trail. The back trail was what he wanted.

He had to say to himself gravely:

"This here's the mountain at my back. That would 'a' been on my right comin' up. I gotta keep it on my left, goin' back."

He made his calculations and crawled forward, but presently his hands shot over a ledge and grasped at empty moonshine.

His senses cleared. He found himself lying on the verge of the cliff.

"That's kinda funny," said Jimmy. "Like walkin' in your sleep."

Then he managed to turn back down the trail and to crawl along it. He could not go rapidly. The injured foot had a way of dangling and dragging like an anchor behind him.

He lay flat to rest. The wind blew the icy chill up his trouser legs, and under his coat. The snow sent its cold upward, reaching into his vitals with a hand of frost.

Twice and again he struggled before he could get to his hands and knees.

"I gotta keep goin'," he said to himself, over and over. "I gotta get far enough so's he won't find me."

So he pushed himself forward.

He dared not lie down and rest again, for he felt that he might not have the strength to start forward after a pause.

Then it seemed to Jimmy that he saw a light down in a valley, and he was starting for it. But he made very little progress. It increased to a vast flare of brilliance. It dwindled to a small, steady point of light. He felt that he was struggling toward it, but that the wind beat him back, blew him literally from the earth, so that he streamed off, held only to life by one thread, as a kite is held.

Then a flash of sense came back to him.

He found that he was lying on his back. The thin point of light toward which he had been struggling was a star in the

sky above him. He tried to rise, but a numb sleepiness possessed him. He decided that he would doze for a moment.

The thought snapped him wide awake. It was the sleepiness
of intense cold, and if he yielded to it, he never would waken.

This he told himself deliberately, clearly, and then added to
his soul that life, after all, was a fearfully hard march, and
nothing won, at the end, but empty hands, and some sense,
perhaps, of having done one's duty. Therefore, he would
sleep, and let the end come.

Each breath still cut him with a fiery blade, deep and
deeper. But his brain was involved with warm sleep. Out of
the distance, it seemed to Jimmy Green that he could hear a
great voice calling for him. He felt that he already was dead,
and that the voice had come for his soul. Well, he was ready
to go.

He said: "Here I am!" and waited. But he knew that he
had only been able to whisper.

That whisper was enough, it appeared. The voice came
nearer. It was thunder on the air. Yet it had a peculiarly
familiar sound. It was like the voice of Alabama Joe.

Then arms scooped him up.

Jimmy went to sleep.

When he wakened, he felt that he was being carried, with
labor, with gruntings of effort. This was strange, for men
said that the soul was winged, or carried upon the wings of
other spirits to the eternal resting place. He thought it strange,
also, that after death the pain should continue in his lungs,
more fiery than ever.

Then he opened his eyes, and saw above him, dark against
the moon, the face of the Stingaree.

"Joe!" he said faintly. "Whacha doin'? Gwan up your
trail! Me, I'm gunna be fine!"

He was gripped suddenly and with enormous strength
close to the breast of Alabama Joe. That breast was bare.
And Jimmy himself was swaddled in a thick layer of clothes.

"The trail's over. Hang on, Jim," said the voice of Stingaree, panting and gasping. "We're going to get there. Keep
your heart up, Jimmy. D'you hear me?"

"Sure," said the boy. "Sure, Joe. I thought I was dead."

"You'll live eighty years more!" said the Stingaree. "D'you
hear me, Jimmy?"

Jimmy heard, faintly, without interest. He started to answer, but he could not. It was a matter of no importance.

"D'you hear?" came the voice again.

Then he received a stinging blow in the face. He opened his eyes, mildly surprised.

"You yellow-hearted coward!" shouted the Stingaree. "Is this the stuff that you're made of? To crawl off and lie down? To stop fighting?"

"You lie!" cried Jimmy. "I ain't a coward. I'd fight—"

"Fight, then! Keep your eyes open. Don't sleep. Talk to me, talk, Jimmy!"

He talked. He argued. His thoughts trailed away from him. Vaguely he fought and won them back, and he heard the Stingaree saying: "Yes, that's right, I understand you perfectly. Keep on talking, Jimmy. How's your chest? Is there a pain there?"

"Nothin' much," said Jimmy wearily.

"Look!" said the Stingaree. "There's the light. We're going to get to it! Keep your teeth set, old son!"

Jimmy looked, and saw a yellow light. And beside and above him arose a great ragged wall of darkness. It was impossible that any man could have clambered down this, loaded with such a burden as a hundred and twenty loose, inert pounds.

"What is it?" asked Jimmy.

"A house—bed—fire, and food, Jim!"

"You think that's a house light?"

"Aye, Jim, it is!"

"I thought so, too," said Jimmy. He began to laugh. The sound was a whistling gasp.

"What's the matter, Jimmy? What's the joke?"

"Why, it ain't a house," he told the Stingaree. "It's a star. How you gunna get there? Can you walk up the sky, partner?"

He dropped off into sleepiness again. He felt himself shifted violently from one arm to another, and he heard the big man groan with effort.

"I ain't any good, and it ain't any use, Joe. Leave me be where I am. I'd rather it that way."

There was an answer, coming from a distance. He could not hear the words.

Then he heard, dimly, a sound like the creaking of hinges, and a wave of warm air rolled over him. Other voices murmured like a stream all around him. He breathed an odor of hot coffee.

Then he did hear something, that startled him almost back to complete consciousness.

It was the voice of the Stingaree, shouting:

"Darn you, don't you see the kid's dying? Where's there a doctor? For heaven's sake get me a doctor! And—and—"

The voice trailed away.

"I knew it was no good," said Jimmy to himself. "Good old Joe!"

The pain thrust through his breast again. He almost groaned, but checked himself, and set his teeth. Through those teeth he must not let a sound of complaint escape, for already the Stingaree had most cruelly accused him of cowardice.

So he locked his jaws like a bulldog, and summoned from somewhere a shadow of a smile.

"I sort of give out, Joe!" he whispered. "But I ain't yaller!"

CHAPTER FORTY-ONE

THAT SMALL CABIN had in it two ragged, battered, greasy-skinned trappers, and the only fragrance was that of the steaming coffeepot. This was the haven to which Jimmy Green had been brought.

They gave him coffee, a mighty dram of raw whisky, and wrapped him to the neck in thick blankets. He fell into slumber like a stone into a black river. He slept with wild visions, and sometimes he thought that he was breathing fire, and sometimes he felt that he was lost in water.

Out of this sleep he wakened from time to time, fitfully, and found always that he was bathed in a dull flare of smoky light. His head reeled and sang. And in the smoke, forms and faces appeared to him, and he could hear the tinkling bells of dog trains in the white winter, and the distant laughter of the boys at the pool near Fort Anxious.

"Joe," he kept saying, "you better hit the trail again."

The trappers told him that Joe was not there. Joe had gone for a doctor. But he could not understand this. Their talk boomed and broke upon his ears like the roar of distant breakers.

Yet he knew instantly when Joe came back into the room,

and his anxiety broke out in a sharp, complaining voice: "Joe, will you start on the hike? Will you start on, Joe? You ain't gunna let me anchor you here?"

"This is where I want to be," said Alabama Joe, taking his hand. "I wouldn't be any place else. Here's the doctor, Jimmy. He's come up from the village to fix you."

The presence of the doctor was reassuring. It was like the touch of a cool breeze at the end of a tired day. He listened to Jimmy's breathing, from the chest and from the back. He took his temperature, and then retired, and talked in a low, grave voice to the three men. Jimmy was very sick. The boy knew it from the manner of all four. But the fever took from him all apprehension. Life was of no great interest.

He fell asleep again, into dreams even worse than before, constantly rousing with a start and choked gasp, fighting for breath. Then in his hand he felt the hand of Alabama Joe, and the reassuring deep voice of the Stingaree soothed him wonderfully.

The trappers turned in for the night. They snored heavily through the hours of darkness. And when the morning came they wakened and found the watcher still beside the boy.

They looked at the face of the Stingaree, gray with weariness and trouble, and they asked no questions.

They cooked a breakfast. The day waxed.

One of them went off to walk the line of the traps. The other remained at the house with the two strangers. He was a wizened old man with a neck that rose from his dingy shirt collar like the red throat of a buzzard from its shoulder feathers. But this old pirate went tiptoe about the cabin floor, gentle as a woman.

"A good, game kid," he suggested once to Alabama Joe.

And the Stingaree looked up with haunted eyes and did not answer.

In the bright prime of that morning a step came to the open door, and into the cabin walked another stranger. He leaned against the door's frame. His hands were deep in his trousers pockets, and the rifle he carried remained on its sling behind his shoulder. But the old trapper looked at him with rapidly blinking eyes, for he saw the uniform of the Mounted Police.

The Stingaree knew that a stranger had entered, also, but he did not so much as lift his head from staring down at the sick boy.

"Hullo," said Mounted Policeman Charlie Dyce.

"Hullo, Charlie," said his long-hunted quarry. And still he did not turn his head.

"How's the boy?"

"Betwixt and between."

Charlie Dyce walked to the side of the bunk and glanced down at Jimmy. He laid his hard hand on the hot forehead of the boy and left it there a moment. Then he stepped back without a word.

No one would have recognized him as the dapper youngster who left Fort Anxious those weeks before. His starved face was set with new lines, deeply etched. His lips appeared to be sealed together, as though he had not spoken for many days of pain and suffering. The Stingaree looked sternly, calmly, at him, and then turned back to the boy.

"You can step outside and see how the weather is, old-timer," said Dyce to the trapper.

The other went instantly, still tiptoeing, but not from fear.

When they were alone, Dyce said: "Well, how did it happen?"

"He had a fall," said the Stingaree slowly. "He was pulling down my rifle, just when I was about to let daylight through Parker—after Parker had shot the dog. Two murders I have against Parker, Dyce!"

"The dog isn't dead," said Charlie Dyce. "I sent up for him, and he was lowered down the cliff. You can't kill that brute with a mere bullet through the head, it seems! At any rate, he has an appetite this morning, but seems to prefer raw man to moose meat. He's back in the village."

Stingaree made no comment on this and expressed no pleasure. He merely rubbed a hand across his forehead.

"I knocked the kid away. He dropped over the ledge of the cliff. Sprained his ankle. Had to carry him, and I suppose that the wind knifed him to the bone, without exercise to keep his blood stirring. Then last night he took himself off my hands and crawled away from the camp I'd made."

"You a married man, Stingaree?" asked Dyce.

"No."

"No children of your own, eh?"

"No. What are you driving at?"

"Aw, nothing." Then he added: "We'd given up the chase and turned back, Stingaree. I was going to cut across the

170

mountains by myself and go up the Yukon. Wasn't that the way you minded to go?"

"No," said the Stingaree. "I was bound for Vancouver."

"You were taking the easy way? I thought it would be the hard one! Well, I can thank the kid for taking me to you, at last."

The Stingaree said nothing at all.

"Well, it was a good long march, Joe," said Charlie Dyce. "And you played a fair and square game. We found your sign down by the camp. Where you'd followed Parker in after he shot Awaskees."

"Was that Parker, too?"

"Yes."

"Did you bag Awaskees?"

"No, he got past us down the river. He must have blown the bullets aside; Butch and Parker fired so many at that canoe. But Awaskees is safe home in his own country by this time, I suppose. I'm glad of it. The whitest Indian in the world—that Awaskees."

Again the Stingaree said nothing. He took out two revolvers and a knife and laid them on the floor.

"There's my battery," he remarked. "You can put leg irons on me, too, Dyce. But let me stay here with the boy. That's his one chance of living, I'd say."

"Listen to me," said Charlie Dyce. "Parker and the other two want your scalp. If they spot you here, they'll never rest till you're a dead man, Stingaree. I'll go head those three brutes off and take them back to the village, and I'll wait there till you show up. Is that fair?"

Loweringly, the Stingaree stared at the man of the law. Never before had he been trusted in this manner. But at last he held out a hand. Cordially, Charlie Dyce took it and then stepped to the door.

"I'll send up some chuck for you," he said. "And remember, old fellow, if you save Jimmy Green for us, you've saved the finest boy that ever stepped out of Fort Anxious."

He waved, and he was gone, while the Stingaree turned his head and looked like one stunned after the retreating figure.

Down the sunlit valley went the Mounted Policeman, his hands still dropped into his trouser pockets, and by the lilt of his shoulders as he walked, the Stingaree saw a great truth for the first time—which is that there is even more freedom inside the law than there is outside of it.

He turned back to the boy.

Cruelty, and a fixed hardness of heart, and an animal sly cunning, had been his chief characteristics when he first met Jimmy Green, but with a strange fire the boy had tested and proved him, until at last the criminal could look inward, and there he recognized none of his old self, but a new soul was in his body, and a new heart beat in his breast. He had found in the world something of a value too great to be had by trickery or cheating. It was worth infinite sacrifice. It was worth death. It was the faith which binds man to man the world over. So Jimmy Green had been bound to him, and he was bound to Jimmy.

He could hardly believe himself.

Yonder was an open door through which he could walk out into the world and leave behind him all but a remote danger of capture. Yet he was not even tempted. His duty was there beside Jimmy Green, and from Jimmy he had learned what duty was. It bound him now with a greater strength than iron.

CHAPTER FORTY-TWO

AUTUMN LOADED the trees of Fort Anxious with snow, which bowed the branches and spilled off until the street and the lanes were heaped with white. There was no wind on this day. But the sky was dark, and the evening was dropping out of the clouds like rain.

There was one cheerful spot in the town, however.

On the western side of the bridge which joined the two halves of the town there was a great battle with snowballs in progress. The forces of the east, led by redoubtable Mickey Dugan, had charged again and again. They had cleared the bridge at last. They had advanced into the precincts which were sacred to the gang of Jimmy Green, and there they held their own with ease, shouting insults, declaring that they were kings of the tower. Now and then the adherents of Jimmy made a half-hearted attack, but they were met with hard-packed balls of the snow, driven home with all the force of strong young arms.

"Where's Jimmy? Where's Jimmy?' cried the afflicted and leaderless clan.

"Aw, he's gone and got growed up!" was the answer. "He's been in the newspapers and everything."

At just this moment of indecision on the one side and of crowing triumph on the other, a small, compact band of boys slipped unobserved along the western bank of the stream. There were four big fellows in front, one step before the others, and to the rear came four more smaller lads, burden bearers, spear-carriers, they might have been called, for their arms were heaped with snowballs.

This new division, coming up through the mist, suddenly charged home. Hard-hurled snowballs, weighty and big as a boy could throw with convenience, went crashing and dashing among the east side gang.

Mickey Dugan, wisely holding himself with a few of his best men in reserve to meet just such an emergency as this, came hurrying off from the bridge with a yell of fury to counter-attack, but they were met with a blinding volley. Mickey, fairly hit upon the end of the nose by a snowball that hurt like a solid cake of ice, reeled away, clasping his nose with both hands. His chiefs were almost as badly handled.

Then two great things happened at once.

Cracking Thunder, an Ajax in the fight, stubbed his toe and fell flat, and at the same instant the whole party of the west side band raised an enormous shout of "Jimmy! Jimmy Green!" So yelling, they swarmed in to the attack.

There was no resistance.

The Duganites were swept off in a single rush. A dozen remained as prisoners, to recant their political faith and form a new allegiance by force, or else to endure the most fiendish tortures that Jimmy Green's Indian brain could devise.

Mickey Dugan himself was seen fleeing headlong, while a pair of ambitious champions of the Green party pursued him.

The rout extended all up the east side. It advanced all down the street. With howls and yells of terror, the Duganites fled into their homes and left the entire town to the open domination of the Greens.

It was a signal victory, a sort of Waterloo for Mickey, an Austerlitz for Jimmy Green.

And it left him free to enter the store of Mr. Bill Carson unseen by any of the enemy, though it was in the heart of his

173

possessions. He walked in and slipped into a corner, where he sat down, panting, red-faced, with an impish gleam in his eyes.

"Hullo, Jimmy, confound you!" said Mr. Carson, from behind the counter. "Come back here and give me a hand, will you? Jimmy, me boy, give me a hand reachin' me things. Doncha see that they's a crowd of folks in here?"

Jimmy Green obeyed reluctantly. He did not like service of this sort. It caused him to pass in review under the eyes of too many irate householders and their wives.

He had come back to Fort Anxious a great man, and more than a boy. The details of his march with the Stingaree were upon all tongues. And it was even said that the notorious Stingaree, now in prison, was well treated for the sake of the kindness and faith which he had shown to the boy, and which the boy had shown to him. But Jimmy's period of good fame was not long. Soon he again was scattering a train of black eyes and of wounded noses behind him. His own right eye, at this moment, was a beautiful green and looked like a patriotic badge. The glories of Jimmy and his good fame were forgotten even in the store of Bill Carson where, at the back of the shop, on a special dais near the stove, lay the mighty bulk of Mishe Mukwa, recovered from his wounds, and now kept in gloomy prison. In this store, one would have thought that the memories of Jimmy's feat would have bulked big in all minds, and so they had, in the beginning, but now wrath had filled up the cup. It overflowed at the sight of Jimmy.

"Jimmy Green," said a stern-faced matron, "wasn't it my own little Johnnie that come home to me with his eyes nigh ruined into his face, and you that done it?"

"I dunno," said Jimmy, ladling out two pounds of rolled oats.

"You dunno! Would any other boy in your crowd be man enough, then, to do such a thing? And ain't he inches lighter than you?"

This accusation roused Jimmy to defense, though long ago he had learned that it was folly to defend oneself from grown-ups.

"We weighed right yonder on them scales," said Jimmy, "and I was two pound more'n him. He called me a Cree half-breed—then he wouldn't fight. I had to tie one hand behind my back. I never seen such a yaller good-for-nothin'."

There was a yowl of rage, and the good lady charged

around the end of the counter and came down to crush the boy. But Paula Carson stood in the path, and the sight of her white face, pinched with sorrow, and of her eyes, wide with suffering, stopped the avenger. She backed out. Her big boy, she vowed, would knock Jimmy into the middle of next week.

"I'll lick him too!" yelled Jimmy. "I'll meet him tomorrow on the bridge. You tell him!"

The crowd of buyers roared with delight. There was not a man in the lot that did not straightway vow to be present when that encounter made history.

Then other accusations followed.

He had stolen a certain pair of pumpkin pies, put to cool in a window. He had dropped a cat on the hot top of a stove during Friday evening singing at the church. He had iced a half of Turner hill, and Mrs. Turner had skidded down it with loud howls and ruined dignity.

The evening crowd dissipated, at last. The three were left alone, and Jimmy went to sit on the shoulders of Mishe Mukwa and rub his knuckles through the bristling mane of the wolf dog.

"He's gunna have your heart out, one of these days," said the grocer.

"I don't mind him growlin'," said Jimmy. "It's kind of like—"

He stopped short, for Paula had winced. She always did. There was no strength in her, who had appeared so independent, and free.

A quick, light step came at the door, and in strode Awaskees, looking thinner, taller, more dignified than ever. He had under his arm a newspaper, and this he spread upon the counter and showed to Paula Carson.

"I met the mail," said Awaskees. "He is coming on with letters, more slowly, but he gave me this paper to take ahead to Fort Anxious."

He stood back in a corner, smiling, in great excitement.

But Paula made very little headway before she cried out: "Daddy, they've pardoned Joe!"

"Read it, Paula!" cried Jimmy.

But, to his disgust, she sank into a chair and began to weep. Mr. Carson snatched up the paper. He was hardly better. He only gave out a few words and phrases here and there, shouting them loudly, then reading on breathlessly to himself, in between:

175

"Good behavior—model conduct—parole, parole!"
He steadied himself. "Here's what:

" 'Because it is believed that faith and truth have a greater meaning than the law, and that loyalty is a virtue which can be taught by such honorable action as the devotion of the three men—Awaskees, a Cree Indian of Fort Anxious; James Green, of the same town, and Joseph Wedell, of Alabama, alias the Stingaree; because of virtues shown to one another, and worthy to be remembered; and because of a conviction that the above-mentioned Joseph Wedell is now fit to take place among the ranks of his law-abiding fellows—' "

"Hey," shouted Jimmy, "whatcha think about that? Joe is gunna come back to us. Lookit! Lookit, Mishe Mukwa!"
The great dog had started up at the word, and, as though he understood, he growled softly. That was his nearest approach to a dog's whine of joy.